BOA
EDITIONS LTD

THE OK END OF FUNNY TOWN

WINNER OF THE BOA SHORT FICTION PRIZE

D0103876

THE OK END
OF FUNNY TOWN

stories

Mark Polanzak

AMERICAN READER SERIES, NO. 34
BOA EDITIONS, LTD. ⸺ ROCHESTER, NY ⸺ 2020

First Edition
20 21 22 23 7 6 5 4 3 2 1

For information about permission to reuse any material from this book, please contact The Permissions Company at www.permissionscompany.com or e-mail permdude@gmail.com.

Publications by BOA Editions, Ltd.—a not-for-profit corporation under section 501 (c) (3) of the United States Internal Revenue Code—are made possible with funds from a variety of sources, including public funds from the Literature Program of the National Endowment for the Arts; the New York State Council on the Arts, a state agency; and the County of Monroe, NY. Private funding sources include the Max and Marian Farash Charitable Foundation; the Mary S. Mulligan Charitable Trust; the Rochester Area Community Foundation; the Ames-Amzalak Memorial Trust in memory of Henry Ames, Semon Amzalak, and Dan Amzalak; the LGBT Fund of Greater Rochester; and contributions from many individuals nationwide. See Colophon on page 196 for special individual acknowledgments.

Cover Design: Sandy Knight
Interior Design and Composition: Richard Foerster
BOA Logo: Mirko

BOA Editions books are available electronically through BookShare, an online distributor offering Large-Print, Braille, Multimedia Audio Book, and Dyslexic formats, as well as through e-readers that feature text to speech capabilities.

Library of Congress Cataloging-in-Publication Data

Names: Polanzak, Mark, 1981– author.
Title: The OK end of funny town : stories / Mark Polanzak.
Description: First edition. | Rochester, NY : BOA Editions, 2020. | Series: American reader series ; no. 34 | Summary: "Fantastical award-winning short stories that use humor, curiosity, and new twists on familiar situations to explore the boundaries of human connection"— Provided by publisher.
Identifiers: LCCN 2019046009 | ISBN 9781950774050 (paperback) | ISBN 9781950774067 (epub)
Classification: LCC PS3616.O5575 A6 2020 | DDC 813/.6—dc23
LC record available at https://lccn.loc.gov/2019046009

BOA Editions, Ltd.
250 North Goodman Street, Suite 306
Rochester, NY 14607
www.boaeditions.org
A. Poulin, Jr., Founder (1938–1996)

For Alle

Contents

4.
EXPERIENCE SURREAL TIMES!

1.
MEET FABULOUS STRANGERS!

Giant

The surprisingly few eyewitness reports stated that the giant walked, more or less, up Main Street from the west, stepping on the pavement and sometimes in patches of trees in parks and backyards, just before dawn. He stopped in the square, choosing to sit in the brick courtyard of the city hall, and leaned back against the big stone church, blocking off traffic on Elm and Putnam. Authorities discovered that he had successfully avoided stomping on parked cars and most of the city's infrastructure, but that many swing sets, water fountains, jungle gyms, basketball hoops, grills, and gardens had been "smooshed." No one knew if any birds or squirrels, likely sleeping in the parks and backyards, had been flattened.

The giant was still sitting in the square in the morning. A crisp and blue Monday morning in September. We found police cruisers and fire trucks parked with lights flashing in a two-block radius of the giant. Residents of the buildings within the zone were evacuated. Businesses were cleared and shuttered. There wasn't a TV or radio station broadcasting anything but news of the giant. Live footage from a helicopter aired endlessly. The giant was taller than the city hall, the stone church, and the apartment buildings, even while sitting. Few of us saw him erect. He wore baggy tattered brown pants drawn by a red rope, an ill-fitting faded green shirt, and no shoes. He was human. He had human feet. Human hands. A brown satchel was strapped around his torso. He occasionally reached into the satchel to remove handfuls of giant berries and something else that crunched and echoed throughout town. He had long, stringy blond hair that fell on either side of his face, down to his shoulders—except in back, where a few strands had been pulled and tied up with a giant red band. No one had heard him speak. No one, as far as we knew, had attempted to communicate.

Since the giant seemed to have purposefully avoided crushing our homes and cars and had made no indication that he wanted to hurt us, we did not panic. Even the flashing lights and sirens did not inspire anxiety. The newscasts were not fear-driven. The reporters were curious. It wasn't an emergency to anyone. It was awe-striking. Eventually, the sirens were silenced. The flashers were shut off. You could hear laughter in the streets. When he reached for more food, there were gasps of joy. Children were held on shoulders to have a look.

The mayor, around three o'clock that first day, was raised up on a cherry picker and handed a megaphone. He said to the giant, "Hello." The whole town was silent, awaiting a response. When, after a minute had passed and the giant had reached for another handful of food, the mayor repeated himself, adding his name, title, the name of our city, and a welcome message. To our great delight, the giant finally acknowledged the mayor, turning to him and emanating a ground-shaking three-syllable reply. But we could not understand. He was not an English speaker.

Professors from the language department of the university listened to the recording, determining that it was not something they had ever heard before. Linguistic anthropologists then went to work on the recording. They were not sure either. Verbal communication was placed on hold.

None of us went to work that first day. No child went to school. Many of us chuckled after remarking that the giant had put things in perspective. Our work seemed small. Our schools seemed small. The giant was all we cared about, and no one disputed it. How could we get our paperwork done with the giant down the street? How could any teacher concentrate on her lesson? There was no way our kids would do math problems with a real, live giant outside.

The influx of reporters and visitors slammed our streets and hotels and bars and restaurants that first night. You could talk with the person seated next to you. There wasn't a chance they'd be discussing anything else. You could talk with anyone on the street. What do you do in a situation like this? He doesn't want to hurt us. He can't talk with us. He just looks tired, don't you think? He keeps sighing and eating. Have you seen that he fell asleep? He sleeps with his head resting on the post office. Did you hear him snore? It sounded like low rolling thunder. Yes, it was soothing. And how he scoops gallons of water from the river with his hand?

Although the mayor had spoken with him, no one had attempted to touch him until the third day. After town meetings to devise the best plan to approach the giant, it was decided that the mayor and thirty policemen would carry flags with every conceivable peaceful symbol drawn on them. A peace sign. A pure white flag. Two hands shaking. The word LOVE. The word WELCOME. Pictures of people waving and smiling. Big flags. Big signs. They would walk cautiously up to the giant. We decided to make an offering. A barrel of orange juice. A loaf of bread the size

of a school bus. We would place these before him and back
away, waiting for him to notice that we were being kind.
Then the mayor and policemen would walk closer and
closer, extending hands and shaking each others' hands
to demonstrate what we meant.

Everything went as planned. But the giant never reached
down to touch anyone. When the mayor got close enough,
he touched the giant's heel. The giant did not notice. This
was frustrating. He ate the bread in a single chomp. He
tossed the barrel of OJ into his mouth, crunched, and
swallowed. He went back to sighing, wiping his brow and
resting.

The giant is not interested in us. He is not curious
about us in the slightest. He eats, drinks, rests, sighs, and
sleeps. He has made no attempt to look any of us, save for
the mayor that first day, in the eye. He has not thanked
us for the food. He has not apologized for trampling our
parks and gardens and recreation areas. He has not offered
any help of any kind.

Not long ago, we began to wonder why we were so curious. What, apart from his obvious size, made him any
more interesting than any of us? Why were we constantly
talking about him, for days and weeks on end? Why were
we fascinated every time he reached for his satchel or
scratched his forearm? We all still talked to each other,
but the conversation turned. We had waited long enough.
We wanted to know if anything was going to happen, or
if we were just going to have to live with a giant in our
square. A dumb oaf that caused people to move out of their
homes, that caused the government to move the offices of
city hall and the post office to other buildings. If he were
of normal size, he would be completely uninteresting. He
would be mentally deficient, mangy. We would pity him.

He contributed nothing. He took. He stole. He trespassed. He destroyed. He frustrated and incensed. He was boring.

When we travel, when we mention where we live and people ask, *Isn't that the town with the giant?* we sigh, *Yes.* When we return home, we ask if it is still there. And our neighbors give the sarcastic answer, *Oh, he wouldn't go anywhere, don't you worry.* When we walk to the bus stop, we glance up at him with as much amazement as we do down to our watches. We know what we'd see. We would see a giant, sitting there, eating and drinking. We'd see a tired monster, not interesting enough to even hurt us. We'd see him wipe his brow. Then we'd check the time.

COMPLICATED AND ANNOYING LITTLE ROBOT

Um. It feels silly to admit this, but that little robot I bought was obnoxious. It was supposed to be fun. It's a toy. A really, really advanced (and expensive) toy. But "fun" isn't exactly the word that comes to mind when I think about the events that followed the purchase of that little robot.

First of all, he was way too commonsensical. And I don't mean knowledgeable. The very first day, I was in the kitchen struggling with a jar of mayonnaise when from somewhere near the back of my knees I hear, in that monotone, condescending voice: "Why do you not break the vacuum seal with a knife around the rim." I spun around to look at him. He looked right up at me with unwavering confidence. Those little square red eyes. I wanted one with blue eyes, but they were out. No one wants little square red eyes. Why did they even make them like that?

"What?" I asked it.

"Did you not hear or did you not understand," he said. He continued to stare up.

I had heard, and I did understand. I reached into the drawer for a knife and slipped it under the rim and cracked the seal. The jar opened easily.

After a moment, I heard: "You are welcome."

Second, when he wasn't following me around the house being condescending, he was off fixing things. He tightened the screws on the banister so that it wouldn't wobble anymore; he swept the foyer and vacuumed the bedroom; he reorganized the pots and pans in the cupboard. It was like my place wasn't good enough for him. I didn't ask him for any of that, and I had to thank him when he was clearly doing it for himself.

His anal-retentiveness came to a head while I was watching television and eating a sandwich. All of a sudden I felt it tapping my kneecap. I bent over, chewing, to see the little robot holding out a napkin.

"What the hell?" I said. "I thought you were reading!"

"I am finished. Here."

"What, you think I'll make a mess?"

"Will you not?" he asked without pitching his voice.

I was sure I'd get crumbs all over the place. "That's not the point!" I hollered and stormed out of the room. In the doorway I turned around, sandwich in hand, to look at the little robot. He was still holding out the napkin but facing me. "You know who you remind me of?"

Then came the coup de grâce. That little robot lowered his little metal arm, dropped the napkin on the floor, and told me: "Make a mess. I do not care," while zipping past me so fast I had to press myself against the jamb to avoid getting tripped.

This was followed by the little robot's little martyrdom. He didn't help out. He didn't offer advice. He didn't sweep or take out the garbage. He just knitted quietly all day long. When I asked him to help put groceries away, there was always a little pause before he placed down his needles and stitch holders. He helped, but he was mostly silent. Sometimes amid the shuffling of the paper bags I'd hear, "Do you want me to put the burger meat in the actual meat bin or do you want me to just throw it anywhere?"

"Throw it anywhere," I'd tell him.

And I got it. I knew I had made him feel unappreciated. Trust me, his charade wasn't subtle. So I did try, in my way, to make amends. It's not like I wanted him to suffer I just wanted him to chill out.

One night I knocked on his door, expecting to find him deep into a mock-cable stitch, and I didn't hear a response. I knocked again and heard some scrambling, then "Come in."

I entered cautiously and looked around the room. He stood in front of a towering corner of patterns, his metal hands behind his back.

"Looks like you've really done some work—" The rhythm of the sentence called for saying his name, but I hadn't given him one. I saw his little metal arm quickly jab at one of his little square red eyes. And I swear I heard him sniffle. "You crying?" I asked him, incredibly curious. Could this wired metal contraption weep, or was he mimicking?

"What is it that you want?"

"I was wondering if you wanted to play some Monopoly with me tonight. We haven't hung out in a while. So—"

He jabbed at his eye again. "That would be fun," he told me. Or he asked it. I couldn't really tell.

"Yeah. Fun," I said.

He told me that he just needed a minute to finish up before joining me. I backed out of his space, careful not to break the treaty.

The little robot got Boardwalk and Park Place, but it wasn't enough for my orange and red monopolies. The game was just the setting, though. I had become a little concerned about him. Although he was supposed to be different, and basically everything he did annoyed me, I couldn't help but think that he would become fun if I gave him something he needed. I just didn't know what it was.

So, I asked him: "You clearly haven't been yourself lately."

"Is that a question?" he stated.

"Yes. What's wrong?"

"Oh, nothing."

"Bullshit." I drove my pointer finger into the tabletop. "I am here for you."

"Look: I want to be happy. You want to be happy. We can't be happy unless both of us are happy. So what's wrong?"

The robot passed his thimble token absentmindedly back and forth between his little metal hands. "I feel like," he began, but stopped. "Nothing."

"No, tell me, please." I leaned forward.

"Okay. I feel as though you do not want me here. I feel as though I am incapable of doing what you want."

"What?" I exclaimed while scanning the room. "You are the best, man."

He looked up at me when I called him man.

"Robot," I corrected with a forgive-me gesture. "Seriously. You are great." I knew I was lying when I said this. I knew I wanted to return him. When he was condescending, it was bad. When he was anal, it was worse. Now, having this soul-sucking, moping, needy little robot around was the worst. I just didn't want him to feel bad about it, you know? It wasn't his fault. I hardly read the product description. I didn't do any research. Hell, I jumped in the day after hearing about him. It was me.

"Really," he asked. I think he asked.

"Oh, yeah," I told him.

The following day I was on the phone with the manufacturer, asking about refunds, when it finally occurred to me to ask what they did with the returned little robots.

"What do you mean, 'What do we do'?"

"I mean exactly that," I told the guy on the phone.

"We crush 'em."

"Like they do with cars?"

"Kind of. I mean, the robots are smaller. You know. You have one."

"Right," I said. "And you can't just set them free?"

"What?"

"You, I mean I—I can't just, you know, let him out the door?"

The guy on the phone told me I didn't want to do that.

But I did do that.

I went to the ATM and withdrew five hundred bucks, got a child's sized backpack, filled it up with yarn and some D. H. Lawrence books, and knocked on the little robot's bedroom door.

He said, "Come on in."

He was knitting and goddamn if I didn't see a smile on the LED of his little damn mouth.

"This isn't working."

"How can I fix it?" he asked.

"No. It's not something tangible. It's not screws and mayonnaise jars and stuff. It's not something you touch, but something you feel. And it's real and true and broken. It's unfixable. You have to go."

The little robot stopped knitting. "You want me to go," he stated.

I marched into the room, pulling the backpack with the yarn and books and cash in it from behind my back. "I got you really nice yarn. You remember when you said that you always wanted Icelandic wool? I got it for you. And I have some money to get you started. And. And. And I don't know. I want you to take it and go make a life for yourself."

I held out the offering for a moment while he examined it. He whirred forward and touched the backpack. He looked up at me. Then I dropped it on the floor and ran out of the room, down the stairs, and out the front door, speed walking down the block.

I found a bar that afternoon and drank until the sun set and my brain came back to normal. He was just a robot, for crying out loud. It didn't work out. At least I didn't just return him like every other dissatisfied customer. I gave it a shot. He wasn't for me. I wasn't for him. It wasn't anyone's fault. And I was giving him a whole 'nother chance. Jesus! He was just a little robot.

When I returned home, I tried my best to enter slowly and quietly, but tumbled in drunkenly. After clanging through the doorway, I steadied myself and whispered, "Hello?" I waited to hear the whirring of his gears or the monotone of his robot voice or the clacking of knitting needles. There was silence. I shouted, "Little robot thing?" But there was nothing.

In his bedroom I found a printed note: "I made this for you. Maybe we will see each other again. Sorry I was not good enough." It was resting on a kind-of nice scarf in the center of the otherwise empty space.

I picked up the scarf and wrapped it around my neck.

It was sad. His farewell gesture was an article of clothing I had specifically told him I didn't care for. We weren't meant to be.

For weeks, I reveled in his absence. I loosened the screws in the banister. The pots and pans became a cluttered mess in the cabinet in no time. I swiped crumbs off my lap and onto the rug. I put beer bottles down on the coffee table next to coasters. I threw a jar of pickles into the trash, unable to open it. I tried balancing Monopoly's thimble token on the tip of my finger.

I pictured that little robot wheeling around the streets with a knit cap on his metal head, mittens, and the child's backpack. I pictured him huddled up in alcoves, reading the books I'd given him. I wondered how he was doing, where he'd wind up. Some afternoons, I wondered if it was him knocking on my door.

Months later, I ran into the little robot at the supermarket. He was zipping along with a tiny cart and a list in his little metal hand. I shouted before he rounded the corner to aisle four, "Oh my god, hey!"

He stopped suddenly and turned around. After a second, he whirred slowly my way.

"Hello," he said or asked.

"Hi," I said.

I kicked the floor. He looked down, then back up to me.

"You look the same," I told him.

"You look good," he said.

"So, you're still here in the city?"

"Yes. I am living on Union now."

"Oh. Nice," I said.

"Yes. Really nice," he said.

"With someone?"

"Yes."

"And it's good?"

"Extremely," he said.

I sensed it. I sensed that he wanted to hurt me. "You know that I spared you, right?"

"What?"

"Did you not hear or did you not understand?"

He was so smart. I knew he knew. He paused, then said, "Well. I suppose I should thank you."

"No need." My confidence came back.

"It was nice to see you again."

"Yeah. Nice seeing you." We turned to part ways. But I stiffened and spun back around. "Do you have a number? Maybe we could get together sometime. I don't know . . . for Monopoly or something?"

He just stared at me with those little square red eyes for a minute. "No," he said. "I do not think that is a good idea."

"You're probably right. Better to make a clean break."

"Yes."

And then we nodded awkwardly and waved.

I dropped my basket by the registers and began to walk out without anything I had come for. But I turned around. I ran down the aisles, scanning the space between linoleum and shoppers' knees until I spotted him again, reaching up for a box of angel hair.

I shouted to him and he turned his head. "You aren't even a real thing!" As soon as the words escaped my mouth I felt everyone's eyes on me.

A moment passed.

"Okay," said the little robot, then he turned back and extracted the pasta before whirring away.

Outside, the sun shone on a clear blue day. A seagull shrieked by the big green dumpster. I leaned on the chalky, rough brick wall of the supermarket for a moment, regaining my balance, letting my heartbeat slow down. Then, I took some deep breaths and began walking steadily to where I lived.

GENIE

The genie is still floating there. His translucent red man-like naked torso tapers down to the lip of the bronze lamp's spout. He's enormous. He has had his neck crooked the whole time he's been out, his head pinned to the four by fours on the basement's ceiling. He pushes down with giant wispy red hands from time to time to bend his head back and forth, side to side, around and around, but then when he lets go, he floats right back up and has to crane his neck again.

I am sitting on the bottom step, smoking a cigarette, and carefully tapping ashes through the mouth of the empty Miller can as if needing to keep the basement floor clean. The genie pushes down, stretches his neck, lets himself back up. I exhale and watch for the line of smoke to break when it reaches the genie's wispy see-through form. He can be touched. He can feel.

I haven't made any wishes yet. It's been three days since I released him. He is not a kind being. He is not a vengeful being, either. He is just a being who appears, sometimes, to be upset. I know he doesn't like his head hitting the ceiling. He wouldn't stretch if it didn't matter. So, when he's looking down from up there, he looks like he's in discomfort. But he's never asked to be moved. He's never said a word about it. Although I know the lamp is now too heavy for me to budge, I could maybe think of some way to help. I haven't dedicated any part of my brain to a solution, though.

"Are you uncomfortable?" I finally ask.

"I. Am. Fine."

His voice is so deep that you feel it in your chest. It comes with a force that is startling, scary even. But the frequencies vibrate your muscles in a calming way. He is very loud. Each syllable takes him one full breath, so he speaks slowly. It's wonderful to be shaken by the booming of his words, remembering that he will never want to hurt me. His voice is beautiful. I love listening to him.

My mother died months ago, and this week I began to go through her things. Digging through forty years of basement-worthy items and memories of my parents will take longer than my typical resolve. I found the genie's lamp in a cardboard box along with bottles of spray paint, warped old textbooks from my mother's nursing school, and spools of rope. The lamp stood out, so I removed it from the box, wanting to take it upstairs to a room I was filling with stuff to maybe not trash. After two strides, the lamp was ripped from my hands, slamming down into and cracking the concrete floor. I ran to the stairs and turned back to see the thing jerking back and forth. What I imagined to be red poisonous gas shrieked out through the lamp's lip in erratic bursts. The genie's emergence took a full day—first a gold-braceleted red wispy arm shot out from the spout and struggled for leverage, more shrieks and blasts of red vapor, then another arm, then, after hours of a terrible battle, the genie finally pulled his head and torso up into the world of my parents' basement. The process was long enough for me to become curious more than terrified. It was a horrible, painful birth to witness.

When I'm on the bottom step, I'm out of his reach. He is not strong enough to move the lamp either.

"Did you meet my mother?" I ask him, dropping the cigarette into the can and hearing the last gulp of beer kill the ember with a *tick*.

"No," he booms, the sound filling the entire basement, thick, rattling windows and throwing open dusty books, sputtering their pages.

"I haven't told you about myself," I tell him and wait to see if he cares to hear anything. He pushes himself down and cracks his neck. He lets himself up and folds his red tree trunk arms over his massive red chest. "This is my mother's house," I continue. "She died five months ago, and I was down here, going through everything. Everything she and my father accumulated in their lives. I was going to throw a lot of stuff away, to maybe clean it all and sell the place." I realize I want to talk about my mother and father. I want to show him a photo or something. This impulse comes with guilt. I feel I must acknowledge my parents' lives, really care for the memories now. Before I can move on.

"Do you know everything?" I ask him.

"No," he booms.

When he finally came into full form in the basement, I realized I had been gripping the banister since running from the terrible lamp. He pushed down and slithered his torso around the space, his head and neck slowly scanning the room. His eyes, awesome black rotating globes, finally found me and he slid his great red head even with mine.

He boomed: "You. Have. Three. Wish-shez."

Then he drifted back up to the ceiling.

I clutched the banister. I waited. "How long do I have?"

"For-ev-vor."

I don't know what to wish for. I leave the genie and the basement to get perspective. I drink tall glasses of water and cans of beer, silently, while studying the woodgrain of the kitchen table. I pace on the back deck of my childhood home, thoughts swirling in my head. I smoke contemplative cigarettes. I stare out to the woods, down to the grass, up to the sky, for signs. Day and night. I think about all the times I've made wishes. It was easy in the past, because they wouldn't come true. I didn't truly believe, so it was always possible to think of something. Eyes closed before the faint warm glow of birthday cake candles. Always a throwaway wish before blowing an eyelash or tossing a penny into a fountain. A shooting star. In those split seconds I was able to think of precisely what I wanted. Because I knew what I wanted couldn't possibly come true.

Now, I am coming up empty. I think of benevolent wishes, selfless wishes. I go down to the basement and ask the genie if they are in his power. They are not. Peace on earth he cannot do. Ending poverty. Eradicating diseases. Feeding all the hungry. These are impossible for him. My wish has to happen to me. I think of clever ways to achieve these grand wishes. I search for loopholes. But he cannot grant me the power to create peace on earth. He cannot give me more food than only I could want. He cannot give me will power.

So I continue to sit on the deck and look at the moon as it changes shape, and drink cans of Miller, thinking about the perfect wishes. Three things I won't ever regret. There is an opportunity here that is impossible to miss and impossible to take. I go down to experience the genie's great spinning black eyes and enormous translucent red form and thunderclap of syllables. I lie awake in my childhood bedroom where I used to do so much wishing, for toys, for superpowers, for bicycles, for A's on report cards, for making sports teams, for winning, for girls, for acceptance. I watch TV. I read books. I clean out the other rooms of this house. I replace light bulbs. I go down to stare at the genie, sometimes with a wish on the tip of my tongue, life-long health and wellness or success in my career, or sometimes for someone else to have discovered the lamp. But I force myself to give it more thought. I smoke and try to relax on the deck. I think it all through. I think everything over. And over.

I do not rush. I go to work. I take lunch breaks. I meet up with friends at the bar and talk about their hopes and dreams and jobs and complaints and girlfriends. I play my guitar and write lyrics. I meet a girl and fall in love. A friend dies. I get married. We have children. We have successes and failures. We watch our friends grow. I raise my son and daughter. I travel to Paris and South America. I go to the movies. I go to graduations and weddings. Celebrate birthdays and ring in new years. I come home and sit on the deck and think about what to wish for. I go down to the basement, time after time, but it's too much pressure. I will never be able to go back on my wishes, revise them. I putter around and think. I stare at the night sky and wonder what they should be. But I just can't pick. I cannot choose. But he's always down there, under my home, in the cool dark basement, among the boxes of my family's stuff I never sorted or removed, craning his neck, folding his arms over chest, full of unimaginable power, waiting.

The Mime

Posters

Posters were everywhere in the morning. During the previous night, shadows must have run about under the streetlamps of our small, empty town, slapping posters to brick walls in dark alleys, with the ease of wind blowing paper down the block. We began to find posters in familiar places that were made strange. On the backs of park benches, way up above our heads on the fifth floor of a building—impossible to reach and unreadable—behind boxes of tissue paper on the shelves of our market, on the roofs of overpasses, on the undersides of manhole covers. In all these now new places, the posters sprouted, appeared to us. Some of us found posters inside our medicine cabinets.

The image showed a heavy red velvet curtain draped before a black stage, and a lone white candle beginning to ignite the fabric. The words read: "NIKLAUS ALSEUR: MIME / WEST END THEATER / OCTOBER 13TH / ONE SHOW ONLY." This was the most common poster. But we all heard tell of small differences, changes, anomalies, possible errors, dissimilarities. On one there was no candle. Another showed a candle but no flame. Yet another showed a thin gray line of smoke rising from the wick. One had no curtain but merely blackness surrounding a small fire. One was said to have a headless man in a white suit, and where his head should have been, the creature held the candle, lighting the golden tassel of the red velvet curtain.

As the posters were discovered, their discoverers removed them. We took them to remember the date and time of the show. We took them while glancing over our shoulders. We took them because they could be for our eyes alone. And we carried them under our sport jackets, folded behind our purses. We brought them to our homes and hid them behind suitcases in the closet, under trunks in our attics, inside our great-grandfathers' snuff boxes on our desks, behind loose stones in our cellars. We did not dare tell anyone where. And just like that, the posters were nowhere, and yet everywhere in our town. Taken. Gone. Hidden. But always here.

Research

Many of us did not tell the truth when asked what we were looking for in the subterranean levels of the library. In the stacks with old newspapers and microfilm machines, we casually glanced about, pulled glasses from our coat pockets or lifted them from around our necks, and squinted at pages, dragging fingers over ink, mouthing the words . . . born . . . trained . . . Eze . . . Cairo . . . Information about the mime. We closed the books, sending up dust puffs, and slid the texts back into shelves that we had not visited since childhood, when the library was a quiet labyrinth of sweet-moldy halls. It was pleasant and gratifying to research in our fine library. Some of us brought the books and clippings home. What were we holding there, as we were entering into our foyers? Oh, nothing. It was nothing. And we poured over the articles in our dark studies, late into the night.

Louise's Cellar

A growing number of the women, the wives and sisters and mothers and daughters of our town, began gathering in Louise's cellar at midnight. Louise was an unmarried woman who had traveled to New York and Chicago pursuing a career on stage. She was somewhat of a celebrity, somewhat of a mystery in our town. She kept to herself. She was a tall woman with long, straight, black hair that hung halfway down her back and obscured her pale face. Her lips were like two red worms. She wore emerald dresses. And she taught our town's women to describe. Louise described a box, placing her arms straight out from her sides, head back, eyes sealed, pressing on the invisible walls without moving her hands, placing her long pale arms above her dark head, trying to break through an invisible lid. Our women and girls described the boxes. They learned the craft. They dragged themselves across Louise's earthen cellar floor by invisible ropes. They dusted off and donned invisible sun hats, pulled on invisible, silk stockings, lit long, white, invisible cigarettes. Louise inspected their technique, peering through an invisible monocle, limping between them with an invisible, ivory cane. And our wives, sisters, mothers, daughters were nowhere, doing nothing at all when they returned to our houses, beds, and breakfast tables. They were not doing a thing. No. And none of them recalled and spoke of these nights to one another. Because there was nothing to remember.

Rumor

At our dinner tables, our sons and brothers regaled us with what they had heard at school, in the cafeteria, by their lockers, at the back of the bus, or on the fields at recess. The mime was actually a mute, they whispered. The mime could not talk, and as a boy he learned to communicate without speaking, by describing items, actions, needs, his desires, his thoughts, all with his hands, his body, his facial expressions, and gestures alone. Eventually, he became so deft at pantomiming that he no longer required the material world. He could brush his teeth by simply miming the act. The mime had been a twin of a blind boy, who killed himself. The mime, after gaining notoriety, found his brother dead in their home with a typed letter pinned onto his coat. His brother could never have seen the mime's act, and decided he could not bear to go on living. The mime went into hiding about this time, setting off rumors inside rumors. The mime had disappeared. Some thought that he, too, had committed suicide. Others believed he was practicing his pantomime, day and night, in a pitch-black, windowless cell, developing and honing a performance the world would never forget. The rumors went on. The mime had actually killed his twin brother and faked the suicide. More. Deeper. Darker. He shot his brother with an invisible gun while rehearsing his show. After that, the mime described a river in the middle of the Gobi Desert and floated away to where no one else could travel, erasing the currents in his wake.

We told our sons and brothers not to believe these rumors. We warned them that to lie is wrong. We told our boys to stop talking with those other boys, because it could not have been our boys that invented these wild and harmful stories. Our boys did not believe in such illusions, such rumors, and they could surely tell when something didn't actually happen in the world. These things were preposterous. None of this happened, and they had to know this. Nothing was true. None of this was real.

Tommy's Dream

Tommy Morrow was four years out of high school. He had curly blond hair and a long, narrow, red face. He wore overalls. He worked for the town's parks commission, and he drank with the other men in town at the Rare Duck Tavern every night. He was sweet and jovial. He laughed at our stories. He did not care that he was slightly out of place among the older crowd. He didn't mind not always understanding what it was that our older men reminisced about. He was one of us. He had seen a poster, and had, of course, stolen it away. But since laying eyes on that poster, he had become increasingly quiet. Something had changed in him. He would not laugh with us. He now stared straight ahead, drinking dark beer, looking jumpy. We asked Tommy, finally, what the matter was. And he told us his dream of the mime.

It wasn't a dream about the mime exactly, he explained, but because of the mime. It certainly had something to do with his upcoming show. Tommy was sure that the mime should not perform. Tommy had dreamed that he was blind. He fell asleep, and when the dream began, he could not see a thing. Blackness. Nothing but endless blackness in his dream. In his dream, he struggled to see, stumbled about, knocking into fire hydrants and telephone poles, calling out to anyone who would be around.

No one answered. He could see nothing in this dream. He could only feel, touch—a mailbox, the grass beneath his toes, the rain on his face, the wind picking up his curly hair, the moment of nearly-imperceptible temperature change when a cloud moved over the sun. He could feel his own blinking eyelids. But everything was darkness in his dream. No change in color. He sensed every object, each element in his environment. But no, nothing was there.

We believed Tommy but told him that it was nothing to worry about. Nothing at all. He was fine. He could see perfectly well now, in the waking world. We tried to forget the dream. We eyed each other. We dispassionately and hurriedly drank more beer. Dreams aren't real. They're nothing in fact.

Reprints

The editor of our town newspaper reprinted reviews of the mime's shows from Salzburg and Brussels. One school of thought had already surfaced, had already begun to dominate conversations at breakfast counters, post office lines, market aisles, and chess tables in the park—mimes are antiquated. A mime could not possibly entertain us. The newspaper articles, reviews, reprints—the entire section dedicated to the mime in the Wednesday edition convinced us all to the contrary.

A decades-old review of the mime's show began with the critic, seated behind a woman in a red evening gown, her hair tangled up in several silver barrettes. Halfway through the mime's show, this woman sneezed, then choked, then coughed. She was in the throes of a small fit. She stood to leave. While she stepped sideways down her row, with her back turned to the stage, the mime spotted her and described a yellow water balloon. The mime heaved it toward her. Without the ability to see the mime in action, the woman stopped short, turned around, opened her mouth in a silent scream, wiped off her face, turned again, and marched up the aisle, shaking water from her hands and onto the reviewer's notebook.

The length of the mime's shows varied considerably. Some were expectedly around two hours. Others were cut down to only fifteen minutes, either because of the mime's irritation with the crowd, or frustration with his own performance. Some shows were sixteen hours, describing a day from the moment of waking in the morning light, to falling asleep at the end of the day, to closing one's eyes, to dreaming.

City Folk

All of a sudden, our diners and markets and parks were a little more crowded. Our taverns filled up with men in suits. The porches of our inns and lodges became inhabited by women who wore long dark dresses and sat cross-legged in Adirondack chairs in half shadow. They were from the city, and they had come for the mime. They reminded us that things were changing. Big things were happening all around us. They reminded us that Tommy had withdrawn and seemed terrified most of the time, drinking with a paranoid arm around his bottle of beer. They reminded us that we all slept in homes where posters were kept in secret hiding places. The city folk reminded us that our women went missing at night, performing silent, dark, mysterious, and invisible descriptions. We had a show to attend on the weekend. How had the city folk heard about it? we wondered. But we made acquaintance with them—at the tavern, at the breakfast counter. We introduced ourselves, and they were receptive. Eventually, we all got to talking about the reasons for their visit to our small town: the mime. Some of the city folk claimed to have seen him perform, and that they would not miss another performance for the world. They said that they remembered the times when he played on the big stages of their city. They told us that they would not miss this, even if the performance were on the other side of the ocean. Some of them reported that the mime had not, actually, performed in their memory. The city folk told us that they, really, had not seen his act but had heard from friends or relatives or perhaps ancestors that the show was something not to be missed. They waited, with anticipation and anxiety, the same as we did, for the mime's arrival. Some of them said the shows they had seen were miraculous, but when we asked for details they were cryptic. When we eagerly pressed for insight, they told us, "The mime is an artist, and it is difficult to explain." Or, they claimed, "The mime has a way of showing you the wonder and strangeness in your own life." Apparently, the mime had a way of showing you how to live, how to believe, how to breathe. When the city folk were drunk they shouted that the mime was a treat, that he had arrived in their city, their grand city, and that it would not be new to them, but they were eager to see our reactions—how they wished they could go back and see it for the first time, as we small-town folk were all about to do. But we could tell that they were anxious as well. They skated off at night and muttered to each other. They couldn't sleep, awoke early, and shot looks at everyone in town as the day of the performance drew near. Where was the mime? What did he look like? The city folk knew the answers, they claimed. But they grew eager along with us. He must be in town already, they said. Where would he stay? The inn? It was booked with the city folk. Maybe he was in disguise. Maybe he was one of the city folk. But no—he would be spotted, a man like that. A true artist would not be able to blend in with the rest of us. But perhaps he could pantomime anything; maybe he could pretend to be just about anyone. The city folk drank our drinks to escape their growing terror, ate our food quickly and unmannered, shopped at our stores while spinning around, alarmed, at the tiniest of noises, read our newspaper in our park, with one eye on us. They were always aware of why they had journeyed here. They were here to see the mime. But no—nothing was that big a draw. Don't bother. It's nothing. It was nothing new to them, of course. Just a show. They shrugged. Nothing at all really.

Ticket Sale

The line stretched from the entrance all the way down to the iron gates of the park at the edge of town. A line of people rolling up hills and down into ditches. At the West End Theater, we waited for the booth to open. And when most of us were turned away—residents and city folk alike—there was a large skirmish and much yelling. The theater announced that something would be done to accommodate us. This was mysterious, but the ticket vendors seemed earnest. What could be done?

Those of us with tickets and those of us without tickets separated. The *haves* hopped on bicycles, jumped on the backs of motorcycles, placed lean legs in long dark cars, and vanished home to place the tickets in their secret hiding places with their posters. The *have-nots* wandered the streets aimlessly. We heard the words, "SOLD OUT!" We looked at the sign in the ticket booth, resting between the shade and the booth's window: SOLD OUT! We inspected the sign, reached in through the cut circular hole in the glass to touch the sign. We felt it, shook our heads, and stumbled down the block, then turned on our heels and marched back to the booth, inspected the sign again, and then, after making clicking noises with our tongues, stumbled away in any direction, being struck by motorists, bumping into others without tickets, getting pelted by errant soccer balls. We stumbled through the park, sitting on park benches, blankly regarding tree trunks, pigeons; we leaned against fountains for stability, turned in circles, stared at the great blue sky, and we fell on the grass. Our heads spun. We had no direction now. We strolled the streets at night, under the town's streetlamps, pausing to examine and greet our own shadows, cocking heads, and wondering what those shadows would now do with themselves. We stepped into the tavern and were greeted with silence from the *haves*. We ordered drinks, drank them absentmindedly while staring at our shiny black shoes or the ceiling fans, spinning slowly around and around, and we left, forgetting to pay. We lost our direction. We were jostled again and again from our sleepwalking. Our dreamwalking, as it felt. People shouted at us. "Watch it! Pull it together! Get out of here!" We continued to stumble through the streets, through shops and diners, through the park, in the light of day, in the light of the moon. We did not show up to work. We forgot to eat at our dinner tables. We were no longer of use, it seemed. We were embarrassed and confused. Until. Until! Until the theater announced its solution. After that, we were, we *have-no*ts, going nowhere, doing nothing. After the announcement, no one remembered that we used to wander. Nothing was wrong. Nothing had happened to us—we who slipped from starlight into the dark forests at the edges of our town.

Change of Venue

The theater made a deal with the shops and restaurants. All the businesses would see some of the money from the ticket sale, and the show would be moved from the West End Theater to Main Street. Those of us who had already purchased their seats would have first choice in the new seating arrangement, out in the street. The rest of us would presumably find seats toward the end of Main Street. We didn't mind. We were delighted to have a chance to attend. Now, everyone in town, all the residents and the city folk alike were permitted to be at the mime's show. We returned to work. We ate great big fat gleaming hams at our dinner tables, spent great deals of money at the diners and breakfast counters, slurping coffee and dabbing at the newly upturned corners of our mouths. We returned with good cheer to the tavern, raising glasses, buying rounds. We were back! We were a part of the town again. We had self-esteem and use. We were born again. And everything proceeded as if none of the midnight wanderings, none of the frequent disappearances ever happened. Nothing had happened. We were fine. Now.

Dissent

Some of us were never going to attend. Those of us with
heart conditions or prone to stroke or aneurysm were not
permitted to purchase tickets. It was for their protection.
These were mostly the elderly, who were disappointed, and
some did give protest, claiming that since they had been to
war they could surely see a mime's show. But no. They were
not allowed. For their own sakes. But some of us declared
disinterest from the very beginning. These were our raging,
brooding, dark, disillusioned adolescents. They would not
be duped, as they put it. Our disenchanted young people
had no use for the mime. We handed them tickets in our
homes, and our teens, our dark-haired girls, and cloaked
boys would not take the tickets. They claimed to be above
it. It was a gimmick, a big trick that conned the rest of us
into believing something, and they would not dare believe.
They were too smart. Too smart to be fooled, and they
would not attend. We left them tickets on their desks, on
their closed computers; we tacked tickets to their locked
bedroom doors. If that was their decision, that was their
decision. But we wanted to offer them the chance. If they
changed their minds, we told them, here is your ticket.

But with their youthful conviction, with quite admi-
rable gusto, they organized a protest in front of the theater. Holding up picket signs, they danced in a circle and
chanted: "WHO WILL BE FOOLED? NOT US! WHO
WILL BE SORRY? NOT US! WHO WILL BE FOOLED?
NOT US!" We admired them. We watched them sing and
dance with their dark eyes, their hoods, their youth. They
truly believed themselves. And we liked that. That they
believed they were right and we were wrong. Still, they
had their tickets if they wanted to come. Nothing was

going to harm them, we assured. Nothing was going to happen. It was fine.

The Show

It was marvelous. Turning of evening. Twilight is what it was. The sun was setting straight down at the west end of Main Street, behind the big black stage that stood ten feet high. The glass doors and display windows of the shops and restaurants along the street, with crooked "CLOSED" signs—all of them closed—reflected the orange, red, setting sun. And as the sun lowered, it melted and poured down Main Street, lighting our feet in a beautiful orange and dark red lava stream for a moment before vanishing altogether. The streetlamps lit up, clicked on bright, in domino succession—one, two, a thousand glowing yellow bulbs on down to the horizon. Tall men in crimson uniforms lighted torches at the end of every row of chairs set out on the pavement. We heard rushes of whispers, the squeaking of chairs. Mothers and sisters wore elegant evening gowns of black satin, of silver silk. Our women were walking, sitting, stirring crescent moons on our street. We were men in tails. In white suits with sapphire vests. Platinum rings shone in the torchlight. We watched as boys fiddled with their little bow ties, and girls shimmied in their best dresses and fussed with their French braids. The night was unusually warm. The torches burned us, as we sought our seats down the aisles. Our entire citizenry was here, stretching down Main Street, side by side with the city folk, wearing pearl necklaces, gold pocket watches. Everyone had a queer smile tucked behind flattened lips.

We all felt like one powerful being—our town come

alive! We were people gathering in the heart of our fair town in our best dresses and suits, after preparing in our homes for hours to appear sleek and elegant, comfortable but formal. Louise placed her pale hand in the palm of a man, who kissed her fingers. She crossed her legs beneath her emerald dress. Tommy, with a friend's arm securely wrapped around his shoulders, took deep breaths in his tuxedo and smiled nervously. We spoke to each other in soft voices, voices of respect, and used words as we never had before—as if these were the last words we would ever speak to each other, or maybe the first. If a lady bumped us, searching for her seat, we gestured in slow chivalry. The moon and stars revealed themselves. Of course, they were up in the sky all along, during the daylight, but we could not see them, and we felt that those sparkling white dots in the sky belonged just to our town, for our one evening out on Main Street. The moon hung low, tempting us to touch. Warm autumn evening. This was our place, and we liked it very much. Torches flickering. Crackling. Moonlight. Men, women, children in long rows. Our faces under dancing firelight.

Some of us had work to do at the show. Some of us were standing behind great spotlights on raised platforms positioned periodically above our heads throughout Main Street. Some of us were waiting in the wings of the great black stage, ready to yank the golden tassels, to pull back the curtain. They held on tight, waited for their cue. The men behind the spotlights watched the men in the wings. The men in the wings eyed the men at the spotlights. We, the audience, settled into our seats. We heard whispers. We heard children shifting in their chairs, restless. Then we heard the final squeak of the last person finding her seat. Finished. We took a long deep breath together and

gazed up to the long, high, black stage on Main Street and
awaited our finest guest.

And we waited for several minutes. Long enough for
some of us to risk a cough in the silence. Some of us reached
into our purses, fetching handheld mirrors, quickly ad-
justing our cameos and hair with sharp, anxious faces and
pursed lips. Some of us smiled to our wives and then turned
our gazes again to the stage. Some of us patted our children on the thigh and calmed them. Some of us pulled out
long gold chains attached to glinting gold pocket watches
and glanced with one eye down at the hands. Some of us
looked to the men with spotlights, who stared at the men
in the wings. We stared at the men in the wings, who stared
at the men with the spotlights. Then we sat up straight
once more and waited.

Then some of us whispered. Some of us doubted.
Some of us wanted to know what was wrong. What was
the matter? When was it to begin? Were we mistaken? We
couldn't be mistaken—we were all here, every inhabitant
of the city, even the cloaked and brooding adolescents had
grabbed tickets from their locked doors and arrived late,
bringing with them the insistent elderly with their canes
and wheelchairs, hiding in the alcoves of storefronts. They
were sheepish, but we smiled to them. Everyone was here.
A town as a whole could not make such a mistake: The
performance was tonight. Positively.

The torches whipped in the rise of a chill wind. We
held our lapel flowers and ribbons in our hair. We leaned
into our husbands. We put arms around our children as
a great gust of wind knocked off hats and extinguished
some firelight. Then the wind ceased, and we again stared
at the stage. We stared. We leaned forward. We squinted.
We blinked. We checked watches. We sat and waited. We

cocked our heads. A long, dark, blank stage. The torches.
Our town. The high black empty stage. And we waited.
Somewhere someone let out a clear and loud "Ha!" And
then we stood and applauded. We clapped and whistled
through our teeth. We held our children up over our heads
so that they could see—so they could have a look and remember this moment. We laughed and hugged. We cried.
We shouted. We grew hoarse. We climbed up onto our seats
and applauded—the entire town and its newcomers—until the sun rose up behind us, over Main Street, and, with
its glorious light, showed us all where we were and how
we could perform.

Unidentified Living Object

One day my clone shows up at my door. He's not looking so hot. I hang up on the person from the B-movie memorabilia store and tell my stammering, shivering clone to come in. His ratty blanket falls off his shoulders as he grabs mine, moaning a half apology of some sort.

I guide him with his twisted ankle to my couch. I put the blanket around him again and fetch the tea that I just happen to have on. He nods, shivers, wraps his hands around the mug. My first guess, I mean after immediately jumping to the conclusion that he is my clone, is that he's just some homeless guy who looks a hell of a lot like me. His hair is longer than mine, to his shoulders. He's got a beard bushier than I've ever tried. He's thinner. But, when you see your clone, no matter the prevalence of facial hair or difference in heft, something clicks and you just know that he's made up of the exact same stuff as you.

I'm not a particularly open or generous person, and I wonder what I would have done if it were anyone but, essentially, myself at my door in need of comfort. I imagine the guy who wears those ascots—the guy my ex left me for—how would I greet him? I wonder if this is going to catch on, this door-to-door panhandling. It really works well. On the street I won't give someone tea, or change, sometimes, even when I have it. But if those same people showed up at my door . . . You know, that just might work for those folks. I wonder if they've tried it already, if I should tell them about it. But then I emerge from my thought-vortex and look down from the slowly spinning ceiling fan to my clone, and he's really in bad shape. He's missing some teeth. It's not so much his looks, but his mannerisms that make me so sure he's my clone. He pulls on his earlobe and clears his throat at the same time I do, and the deal is sealed. I draw a bath, light a candle because I'm really caring now, and place my red-and-black-checkered robe on the hamper for him. He whispers an apology as he sinks below the water. I shut the door and put up a hand. *It's nothing. Rest.*

He's had a bowl of soup I reheated, and a grilled cheese, which I made on the spot. I stare at the bowl in his hands, this little white bowl with a blue lip. In a flash, I remember buying the bowl—I stood in the aisle of the massive home-goods store, looking at the infinite array of bowl options. I didn't like the blue-lipped bowl; I chose it for how cheap it was. But it's fine. It's okay. It does the job. That bowl's mine. And I watch this other me dipping bread into my bowl at my kitchen table. He's in a fresh pair of khakis, clean tee, and my old barn jacket that I used to wear all the time in college. It looks good on me, I think, looking at my clone; why did I ever stop wearing that old barn jacket?

All of a sudden, my clone heads for the door with renewed vitality. I try stopping him, and I finally grab hold of his arm. I can see that he wants out. He's furious with confusion or sadness. I ask if he's got somewhere to go while flipping open my wallet and handing him twenty bucks. He walks down the road, turns around, and for a blink I can see myself standing in the halo of soft living room light in my doorframe. I see this real me in his home. Me, from a distance. Am I envious of that guy, with his cozy dwelling and stocked cupboards and little curiosities? Or is he just some random schmuck? Either way, there I am. Here I am, alive. Then, my clone marches into shadows, vanishing.

———

Entering my girlfriend's place is like crossing enemy lines. I have to sneak up on her, or else she'll flake on me. I knock, but obviously she can't hear me over the buzzing of her power tools and blaring of techno-rave. I try the knob and feel something pushing back against the door from the inside. She finally notices me, and I stop trying to enter. I peer through the narrow opening and spy about a dozen flat-screen televisions, showing color-bars and hanging by nooses on the far wall.

"Hold on. Hold on! Give me a fucking second!" I see her run back and forth, in a welding mask, cutting this way then that way. Existing. Disappearing. She doesn't like for me to see her artwork before it's finished. Something clunks on the other side of the door, and it gives. "Okay."

"What's that?" I place my blazer on the hook and point to the TVs.

She yanks a curtain across the room to conceal the mass. "Televicious," she whispers, begrudgingly. She waits. I ponder it. "That's what's fascinating about you, Jerry." She approaches, studying my face. "You don't get it. You simply never get anything I do. It's so fresh." And she's out of sight, in her studio, hiding her projects from me.

Laura's artwork is concerned with busted flat-screen televisions, monitors, personal assistant speakers, computers, and tablets as far as I can tell. I have never liked her stuff all that much. Before I met her, I would joke with my ex about how ridiculous art like that was: conceptual stuff that makes no sense. She hid this side of herself from me when we started dating. She told me she was an artist, graphic designer, but then one day she showed me her portfolio, her real passion, her true self she even said. I was supportive about the collages of wires and circuit boards until she didn't need my blind support anymore. I'm still kind about her pieces, but now she has regular shows, and critics write think-pieces about her messaging. She is happy with me just not getting it. I have become a cute thing. Cute and ignorant. But I'm not dumb, and I think she knows it, too. But here I am. Her dummy.

On nights when she's into her project, there's no room for me. But I watch her float around her place, build her secret installations, and see flashes when she's photographing her sculptures. I eat her Brigham's and hint at streaming movies on properly functioning TVs. I stand most of the time at Laura's. Tonight, she's possessed. She asks me to hand her wrenches and washers while running from room to room. I watch the news with the captions on.

I started living in Somerville three years ago, after I moved out of my ex's in Cambridge. Pushed a town over for rising rent. It's a fine place to live, I guess. Laura's been living here ever since college. She absolutely loves all the artists and musicians. She's from rural New Hampshire, and she's excited to now live in a town with fewer monster trucks than bookstores. Her childhood home is now a gas station. She showed me once. We bought a pack of cigarettes and smoked a couple where she used to sneak them in her brooding youth: her side yard, the parking lot. I worried about the tanks blowing up. She is the first girlfriend I've had since getting the heave-ho by my ex. Right now, though, in her apartment, I try to look at her as if for the first time with snap judgments. I must have had them, back in one second, way off in the past. What does she do? What's she like in bed? The initial wonder—those playful, hopeful unknowns—it's all irretrievable. We know what we are now. An okay thing. I think she thinks we're okay.

When the news ends and the late night talk show starts, it's clear that Laura's not slowing down, so I head off to the D and D for hot chocolate. On a newspaper rack inside the shop, a magazine cover shows two identical lab-coated scientists. The headline: HUMAN CLONED. I ask the girl behind the counter if she knows anything about it.

"I don't just work at this donut hole," she says through blue lipstick. I didn't mean to offend her, but I actually didn't assume she existed outside this moment in time, pouring hot chocolate, now that I'm forced to think about it.

"If you did just work here, that would be fine with me."

"I'm in college. I bet there are thousands of clones out there."

"Really? That many?" I sip my hot chocolate, lean on the counter. "Wouldn't the people who were cloned know?"

"No. Not if they were too young, like zero or something."

The curtain is drawn back from the wall of now powered-off TVs when I return. Laura's sitting on the floor and stretching her back. She has to do this weird stretch where she sits with her butt on her heels and leans back. Every night she does this before bed. It's a weird position, but just something I always see at this point. I put a cup of hot chocolate on the floor in front of her so that she'll smile when she bends forward. I sit on the couch and flip open the magazine.

"I finished Televicious," she says, still stretching.

"Tremendous," I say. I hate it when she's working. The gallery openings are okay though. I'm somewhat of a curiosity for her artist friends. They look at this dude, this me, wondering how I'm at Laura's savvy side. I wonder, too, I guess.

"What are you reading?" She's done with the weird stretching.

I tell her about my clone showing up at my place.

"So, some lunatic could have killed you in your own home and you're reading about DNA splicing?" She takes her hot chocolate.

"No. You should have seen him. He was my clone. He was me."

"I'm not in the mood."

"Have you given any more thought to living together?" I put the magazine down and wait.

"Would your clone have to live with us?" She's not taking me seriously. And I don't want to get sad and hurt again, so I drop it. "You've been reading too much for *Nexus*."

She's talking about my job. I am an editor for a popular science-fiction magazine. We are specific about science fiction: no fantasy. And we don't like it when people confuse the two. There is that much bigger journal, *Fantasy and Science Fiction*, which has set a mixed tone, and we have been fighting that tone with our concentration on sci-fi. We want robots, futuristic computers, colonies on Mars, mad scientists. As I like to define it: if you have a dragon, you're submitting to the wrong place; if you have a test tube, show us the experiment. I see it all—predictive dates of death etched on human skulls, revealed post-autopsy; starfish genes spliced with butchers' DNA when they lop off a finger; little green aliens heralding cures for cancer, but who get killed by humans (heavy, moralistic). I write my own stories, too. I wanted to be a science-fiction writer, actually, but after years of never seeing a single published piece, I made a lateral move to editing the stories of more talented folks. It's okay, though. Really. I get some satisfaction from my work. It's okay.

Our offices are in Cambridge. If mad scientists were to concoct clones and fountains of youth, chances are they'd be doing it in Cambridge, where *Nexus* is, right between Harvard and MIT and, to a lesser extent, Tufts. There are boatloads of discoveries made in Cambridge because of these institutions, and this has probably fueled the sci-fi market, where our contributors take the next logical step after researching the last real-life step that local laboratories have already taken.

Today, I'm reading a submission from Lesley Ofrichter, a writer I've been fighting for, trying to get her published for years now. Her stories all have the same three elements: secret experiment in a clandestine laboratory, the experimental subject escaping from the laboratory, and that secret experimental subject seeking out its creator for a reckoning. It's formulaic, but it works for me. I love them. This one's about a little pink piglet that has been given a red-tailed hawk's wings. Zachary, the secretive scientist, is a ladies' man. When the piglet bursts out of its cage and flies through the laboratory window and on over to Zachary's house, his latest flavor-of-the-month lady friend is trying to get Zachary to talk seriously about living together. He's thinking, *when pigs fly*. And then, the gruesome, flying piglet crashes through his window, and Zachary makes serious changes to his womanizing ways, reinvents himself completely.

"Jerry," Pratt, the head editor, is calling me into his office. Pratt has final say on everything. "Do you have something to send my way for the November issue?"

"I have a new Ofrichter story—"

"God, she's still at it, eh? You know I'm not a fan."

I don't do anything. The story's fate hangs in the air.

"I'll take a look, but you have to show me at least two other pieces."

"Of course." I maintain my cool, but I still haven't won, haven't assumed the position of authority. I won't hold my breath for "Porcine Heights." But Pratt will spring for lunch, and it will be fine. Here's me at my job, talking with my co-worker, or my boss, or my intern.

What Ofrichter would write for my situation with my clone is that my clone comes to my house, but he isn't disheveled and in need of help. I would be the one who needs help. And he would fix me, show me the mistakes I made, the changes I need to make. Or my clone would be superhuman, threatening me with cement fists for answers: *Why did you make me?* Of course, in my real life, I didn't make my clone, and I don't have answers for him. I have no idea how he exists. But Ofrichter would have my clone find me again, and in a fit of rage, coax the answer out of me: *I made you to be the perfect me. I made you the way I wanted to be . . .*

———

I'm flipping through a newsletter I get on sci-fi conventions, which has this section in the back for Martian figurines, UFO posters, actual ears of corn from crop circle sites. I haven't been to a basketball game since I was ten. This is my hobby. Here's me looking into the cost of a robot can opener. I hold up a toy flying saucer to the sun coming through the bay window in the kitchen. The phone rings. It's Laura. She's getting her show ready.

"Where is it again?" I ask.

"Porter Square. Behind the big sculpture that you always call the alien satellite."

"You know, as well as I do, that thing is sending up coordinates."

She's not listening. She's with her artist friends at the gallery that's putting up her latest installations. I can hear their turtlenecks swishing in the background. This is the group I mentioned before: the one that I'm a curiosity to.

"Should I bring wine?" I ask.

"No, Jacob has outfitted the whole thing."

"What does the installation mean, so that I can pretend to be hip tonight, honey?"

"Never change, Jerry."

She tells me when to show up, what to wear. I hang up and go back to inspecting the flying saucer. I make a noise with my mouth that I think is a ray gun.

The article on clones says that in the future you'll be able to tell clones from real people because clones won't have belly buttons. I think about this. This minor detail, the no belly button, is horrifying. It's like, I never thought about it, but belly buttons are nature's stamp of authenticity. If all clones were to be missing one ear, one finger, a tooth, if they were all hairless or something, it wouldn't be so bad. They'd be noticeable, but not scary. The missing belly button, though, seems hideous. The belly button doesn't do anything, but to be missing it makes me think that cloning is so unnatural. The missing belly button makes me question my stance on cloning, when I had been so into it before. With *Nexus*. With my own clone and all.

———

Fifteen minutes before I'm supposed to be heading out to the T and on over to the gallery opening, my clone appears at my door. He's doing even worse now. He has a black eye. Dried blood runs from his nose to his upper lip. He's in the khakis and shirt I gave him last time. The barn jacket's left arm is missing. He collapses in my arms, and I half drag, half carry him to the couch, where I prop him up.

I startle my clone when I dab his nose and eye with a moist towel. He flinches and moans while I clean him up.

"Doesn't look good," I say. His nose is blown up, his eye getting puffier. "But, you'll be okay."

"I'm sorry," he moans. It's fascinating: I can hear my own voice. Although it's as if it's me talking after being punched in the throat, I can hear my own rhythms coming out of him. He begins to cry, but I stop him.

"Oh, no you don't. You're going to be fine. Everything is going to be fine. You are just a little bit confused right now. You are going to make it. Trust me. Get up." I stand and put out my hand. I've shocked him, and he stops his little sobs. He pushes up off the couch. I put my hand on the top of his head and then drag it slowly, flat over my own. "Remarkable," I say.

I've got him in the shower, and I'm putting out another suit, tie, and slacks for him to wear to the opening. I knock on the bathroom door, "Come on. We've got to go!" I think that this is tough love. "There's food at the gallery." In case he's angling for a round of soup and sandwiches.

With his hair pulled back into a ponytail, held together by one of Laura's forgotten purple hair elastics, and my suit on, exactly as ill-fitting as it is on me, he looks presentable despite the black eye, which I suggest he cover up with dark aviators. But how does he feel?

"Disappointed. Confused." He's wobbly, and finally he reaches for the arm of the couch and sits.

"What's your name?" I ask.

"Gary." He lightly pinches the bridge of his nose, and when he shivers with real pain, I cringe with the phantom type.

"Gary? I'm Jerry." He nods. I nod. "How did you find me, Gary?"

Gary raises his hands as if under arrest. Then he drops them. "I have no idea where I am. I have no idea how I got here, where I've come from. All I can remember is looking up from a dirt road to this great white light that all of a sudden cut out. I only know my name because it was in my emptied wallet. I've got no clue who I am." He's serious. He's looking right into my eyes, I think, through the aviators.

"You still have a chance to clean up. Every day is a new opportunity, you know?" And I think that if he can read, he could probably do my job. I wonder if he can lick envelopes, work his way up at *Nexus*. But, no, he wouldn't want that. What he should do is write his story. I imagine him as an amnesiac whom I could help retrieve his origins and tell the world.

I decide he's my burden now. I look around my place, at the flying saucer on the shelf, at the magazine on cloning on the coffee table, at the last issue of *Nexus* on the bookcase, the photo of me and Laura on the mantle, taken what seems like a lifetime ago. I look at my clone: me, in the middle of my living room, in the middle of my life.

We must have been a sight on the subway: two identical men in suits, one with shades on at night, his arm around my shoulders, me supporting him when the brakes screech, when the car gathers up momentum.

I plant my clone at the cheese and crackers table, pour him a ginger ale, and tell him to just hang here for a minute. There's a massive installation hanging from the ceiling, all cords and wires and computer screens entangled. I spot Laura in the back, in front of Televicious, encircled by men with shaved heads, stylish seeing glasses, women with pink Mohawks and little handbags. I know them. They know me. Laura waves me over.

"Where have you been all my life," she says. I kiss her on the cheek and wave a little wave to the circle of artists. They say hello, but I've obviously stopped their conversation.

"How did you find this mad genius? And, moreover, how do you put up with her?" I think it's Jacob that asks this.

"I love her," I say. Everyone *awwws* at this. I pull Laura away from the group, and they follow me with their ten eyes. "Laura," I whisper in her ear, "I've brought my clone."

She laughs, pushes off my chest. "What?"

"Remember? My clone? I brought him tonight. Look." I point to Gary who's munching on something at the food table. People are giving him a wide berth.

"Who is that?" Laura's done laughing.

"I'll introduce you."

Gary wipes his hands on my slacks and I introduce my girlfriend to my clone. Laura doesn't take his hand when he offers it. She's pissed. Gary goes back to munching.

"This is my night," Laura says, outside on the street. "Are you nuts? Bringing some homeless guy to my opening?" She crosses her arms, sucks her lips into her face. She doesn't see it, clearly, that he is me.

"Laura, the guy's me, and he's had a rough time. So, can you please try to be nice? Try to understand this?" Laura looks over my shoulder. I turn around and Gary's standing in the entranceway to the gallery. He's gazing up at the black sky above the streetlamps. Laura shouts to him.

"Gary? Hey, Gary!" Gary looks at her, removes my aviators. "Gary, what kind of con is this? What do you want from us?"

Gary doesn't do anything. He looks at the two of us, me and Laura.

"Is he deaf, too?" Laura asks me. "Hey, buddy! What are you doing here?" She annunciates each syllable. What. Are. You. Do. Ing. Here?

And I look at Gary, in my suit, the group of Laura's artist friends inside the gallery, staring back out to this little scene we're causing. I see Televicious glowing in the back, a double-helix of monitors and nooses. Laura shouts. "What are you doing? Where did you come from?"

And for a blink, I can see through my clone's eyes. I see me, looking dumbstruck in a suit, standing next to Laura whose arms are crossed on Mass. Ave. This couple. This time. This place. The big alien satellite sculpture behind us in the middle of Porter Square, sending out signals to Andromeda. The streetlight flashing green and red at the same time. Stop. Go. The conical shade of incandescence, streaming down from a streetlamp like a photon tractor beam. Televicious throwing mad, bouncing images over our bodies. The glowing yellow windows of the apartment building across the street going dark, one, then another, then another. Cigarette red cherry burst at a gas station, a childhood home. A laser beam shooting from a policeman's flashlight into an alley, illuminating the ankle of a metal giant. Cars sailing, floating, flying west, east through the world like spacecrafts. A shooting star. The flutter of a specter between us. A little green alien diving into a trashcan. A secret experimental beast shaking his cage. Roaring. A broken vial. A puff of smoke. Neon blue liquid, dripping down a sewer drain. A robot's "ON" switch. Square red eyes. Numbers etched into bone. A stork. Ear of corn. Crop circle. Black cat. Blue lips. Purple and orange border on coffee cup. A new constellation. Black hole. Umbilical wires and circuits. Cave drawing. Installation. Post-apocalyptic ashen rubble. A blue lake on Mars. Telescope. Worm hole. Time machine. Stegosaurus. Sugar on tongue. Smelling salts. Sun spot. First fire. Flying saucer. Tombstone. Clay. A daisy. Sea foam. My father, me a sparkle of dancing light in his eye, gazing down at my mother in their marriage bed. Laura stretching. *Nexus.* My blue-lipped bowl, spinning and spinning. Waves. Eons. Boulder. Pebble. Crow's caw. Belly button. Man in cab. Woman on phone. Anyone. Anywhere. A proton. A neutron. An electron cloud, firing madly. A hydrogen atom. A deafening big bang. A blinding burst of white light. A sharp gasp of oxygen.

And I say, "I have no idea."

2.
TRAVEL TO FANTASTIC PLACES!

The OK End of Funny Town

When I peeled myself off the Velcro wall, I collapsed on and snapped in half my arrow-thru-the-head gag. It was not funny.

Letting the Krazy Glue set, I reloaded the bed catapult, clipped on my yellow squirting lapel flower, and fetched my googly-eye glasses.

In the wavy bathroom mirror, I saw that the glue job didn't pan out. The arrow tilted down. I picked the thing off my head and wrapped it in the pages of comic strips. I went through my closet: fake bald head, fake Mohawk, alien antennae, horns, elephant nose, oversized ears. I settled on the blue, red, and green beanie with the purple pinwheel on top. But I knew it wouldn't be right. It wasn't what I needed. When you've got your heart set on an arrow-thru-the-head gag, all the other panoply pales. I twirled the pinwheel and felt hollow.

I hurried through the morning: bug juice all over me from the dribble glass, the fly-in-the-ice-cube bonking me in the nose; a handful of peanuts from the spring-loaded snake canister. Then I slipped the injured arrow-thru-the-head gag into my bottomless backpack and rode the zip line out into the streets of Funny Town, determined to buy a replacement. Dead set on finding it.

Have you heard the one about the guy who walks into a bar . . . and it hurt? The one about the drunk who rubs a lamp and a genie grants him three wishes, and the guy wishes for a glass of beer that can regenerate when he finishes it, then the genie says, "Hey, the other two wishes, buddy," and the guy says, "I don't know, just two more like this, I guess?" The one about the guy sitting on a bench with a box, who says to the guy next to him, "If you can guess how many kittens I have in this box, I'll give you both of them?"

They're tired, but there's a joke maybe you haven't heard. And it goes like this: There's this guy who moved to Funny Town after his fiancée left him at the altar, and now he's taking small gigs in jokes. When the guy goes to sleep, right before he closes his eyes, he wishes he could cry again, but he can't because it's impossible in Funny Town. And when he tries to weep, sob, moan, in the dark, in his tiny quiet moments of privacy, instead he lets out a guffaw that echoes across the world.

That one's still in the works. It's my original. We all have to come up with an original. Taxes.

After an admirably placed oil slick and bed of thumbtacks, my unicycle was useless. I slipped on my oversized red thumb and hitched a ride with a rainbow-painted Beetle.

"Where you headed?" asked the driver.

I could barely breathe, packed between the eleven clowns in the backseat, but managed to wheeze, "Acme Clothes."

"Holy Smile," shouted one of the clowns. "That's on the other side of Funny Town!"

"Can't get you all the way there, buddy," the driver told me. "But close."

I thrust my hand into the cockpit and formed an OK sign. I shifted around and patted my backpack, feeling for the arrow-thru-the-head.

"What you need at Acme?" I couldn't tell which clown was interested, my face pressed to gigantic red shoes.

"Arrow-thru-the-head gag."

Paisley kerchiefs and bowling pins went flying around the car, along with hoots and hollers.

"A classic!"

"Oldie but a goody!"

"Like there's an arrow stuck right through your HEAD!"

I couldn't laugh. "I broke my old one," I said.

The car fell silent.

"I'm going to get a replacement," I said.

"And how do you feel about that?" It was whispered.

"I don't know. I've never felt quite like this. It's like there's just nothing inside me."

Suddenly, the gigantic red shoes, the billowy polka-dotted pants, the frizzy rainbow wigs, they all vanished, and I fell to the floor. The clowns had stacked on top of one another, giving me room on the seat. I regrouped and stretched. They stared at me. I caught the driver's over-sized sunglasses in the rearview, and then he bent the mirror away from me.

"You keep that on the inside," said one of the clowns.

I patted my backpack.

"We're all crying on the inside, man," said the driver.

But then there was gridlock. All the clowns leaned out the windows and honked their noses at the other clowns and some penguins that were crossing the street, caught up in the mix.

The honking was deafening. "That's not going to fix anything," I shouted, covering my ears. Then, I slipped out through the trap door.

———

But after the guy lets out the guffaw through the entire world, he gets out of bed, clicks on the nightstand lamp, reaches under a loose brick in the wall, and removes a cigar box. Inside the box are yellowed photos with turned up edges. The photos are of a man and woman cuddling a baby. The man and woman are dead now and the baby has grown up, and he looks at the photos.

But, no. In fact, his parents are alive and well, living across Funny Town in an inflatable moonwalk. And the grown-up baby wishes they were dead. And he doesn't know why. When he thinks of his father shaking other men's hands with a buzzer strapped to his fingers, the guy crumbles onto the floor, activating a set of chattering teeth and slowly deflating a whoopee cushion with the sound of a remorseful French horn.

———

After sliding down the big blue slides and silver firemen poles, and slipping on banana peels the rest of the way across town, I read the sign in front of Acme: CLOSED. BE BACK HALF PAST A FRECKLE.

I removed the arrow-thru-the-head gag from the comic strips I wrapped it in and put it on. In the windows of Acme, I studied the down-turned arrowhead.

"Pssssst," I heard from the alley. I whipped the gag off my head and scanned the street.

A guy in a gorilla suit and a trench coat waved me into the darkened corner, glancing around wildly.

"You need something?" he whispered, thrusting his crazy gorilla eyes close to mine.

"Arrow-thru-the-head," I said, and slid my foot back.

Then the guy flipped open his trench coat and went riffling through his hidden pockets. He pulled out a metal briefcase and clicked it open under my nose. And there it was: an arrow-thru-the-head gag, delicately cradled by orange foam.

"It's the latest model. Real nice, man," said the gorilla-suit guy. He placed the briefcase on the ground and eased the thing out. He put it on my head. "The arrow slides, man." He pushed the feathers of the arrow, and the tip jutted farther out. "It's like you're sliding the arrow through your HEAD!"

I picked it off and slid the arrow back and forth. "Pretty cool," I admitted.

"Pretty cool? This shit isn't even declassified yet."

I absentmindedly twirled the gag in my hands. The gorilla-suit guy chomped a banana. "It's not right, though," I said. I handed the thing back to him.

"You'll never want your old gag after you've had this one, man." He demonstrated the gag again on his own furry head.

"Yeah. It's just not what I'm looking for."

He clicked the briefcase shut, threw it into his trench coat. "You don't know what you want, bro." Then he scaled the fire escapes and swung out over the rooftops.

———

Next, the guy goes to the kitchen, pours himself a glass of his finest bourbon, and sits down to write a suicide note.

He writes that he can't take it anymore, all the laughter, all the good times, all the sunshine and love. He writes that he's going to take his own life because he's no good for this place. He's only a minor joke, not anything that this town would miss. He writes that he does wish everyone well, but he knows that everyone will be well, which is partly what is making him kill himself. It might make a decent joke. Maybe a funny anecdote, at least.

He heads into the bathroom and cleans himself up. He shaves. He lights a cigarette and sits down at his dining room table. After his final drag, he puts the smoke in the ashtray and raises a gun to his head. He whispers goodbye and pulls the trigger. A flag bursts out from the nozzle. It reads: BANG.

***

At noon, I headed to the bar.

I waved a hello to the rabbi and asked the frog on his shoulder how things were going. I avoided the ostrich and the cat with the sunglasses and their master, the guy with perfect change all the time. The duck was already getting to the bartender, asking if he had "any grapes? any grapes?" The psychiatrists took turns asking the light bulbs if they really wanted to change. I shook my head at Kowalski with his handful of crap, repeatedly shouting, "Look what I almost just stepped in!" Santa and the Easter Bunny shared a laugh at the blondes, who scrambled for the dollar on the floor.

Then, right before I walked into the metal bar, at forehead level, in front of me, I took a closer look. I noticed that the rabbi's Torah was ripped; the frog was looking malnourished; the ostrich and cat with the sunglasses were on choke chains; the guy with perfect change all the time was nursing his "beer," but eyeing the top-shelf stuff; the duck and the bartender had their fingers crossed; the psychiatrists' pens were filled with invisible ink; Kowalski was inching toward the door; and the blondes were starting to show.

I walked into the bar, and it hurt. As I fell, I shouted out, "How can you laugh?" But then I was seeing fireworks, stars, birdies.

When I awoke, I ordered a beer and eyed the lamp. I took a swig and rubbed the thing. The genie materialized, giving me a little wave. He stretched.

"You got three wishes," he yawned.

"I want to know why I want my arrow-thru-the-head gag," I said.

Everything stopped. All eyes turned to me. The genie shrugged to the bartender, who folded his arms. And the genie, my old partner, snapped his fingers.

———

I came to on a dirt road. The world looked gray and brown, dusty. I adjusted my googly-eye glasses, which Slinkied into themselves and formed lenses. I fiddled with my yellow squirting lapel flower, which folded and bloomed into a sunflower. I spun the pinwheel on my hat, and it flew off, a butterfly. Gone into the sky.

I flipped my backpack off and withdrew the arrow-thru-the-head gag. It was still broken. It wasn't morphing. It wasn't going anywhere. I put it on, and it remained broken, there on my head.

A pickup truck rolled up the dirt road, spraying dust behind it. It clattered to a stop in front of me. A beautiful, sad-eyed girl stepped out.

"Where you headed?" she asked.

"I don't know where I am." My legs gave out, and I knelt down.

She took up my arrow-thru-the-head gag. I watched her as she flipped it around, studying it. "What is this doing on your head?" she said.

"It's a joke. Like you got an arrow right through your head." I smiled weakly.

"No. No," she said. She reached around my chest, curving the arrow to look as though it were stuck through my heart. "That's where it goes in these parts. It's not fun."

She touched her breast. I saw a bloody bandage. "Are you okay?" I asked.

"No, but who is? Where you need to go?"

I stood up. "I need to go where there's honesty, pain." I shuffled my feet, felt stupid.

The beautiful girl put her hand on my shoulder. She cradled my head. She pulled me into her and squeezed, bending and breaking the arrow. We kissed. I felt her sadness. Oddly, I wanted to help her. I wanted to tell her a joke, make her laugh, cover it all up for her.

I felt my chest heat up. The plastic arrow straightened, hardened into a blade. It shot cold through us. Stabbed, we stuck together, in the big lonely world. Finally, for one glorious instant, everything raged cruel and alive.

Our New Community School

Subject Matter

In the beginning our New Practicals catalog threatened no one. Despite its newness, despite its never being seen before in an adult educational institution, people were not shocked, were not appalled, weren't even suspicious, at first. The courses were "accessible." Our students—all men and women choosing to continue their education after obtaining their BAs and BSs and settling into careers and families—remarked that we should have taught these subjects all along. One such New Practical offering— SWT/110: Staring at Walls and Thinking While Seated— was a smash hit. Within days of its appearance on the website, the course had filled. We scrambled to find an additional instructor to teach a second section. The fact that this course was not offered at any community school, that it did not fit into a traditional pursuit—English, Music, Biology, or Business—did not bother anyone. Yes, we saw it as a gimmick. Yes, we understood that there was no traditional academic value in sitting and staring at walls and thinking. But we saw that folks in the community were struggling with the undertaking of Staring at Walls and Thinking While Seated, and as educators, if we could provide an expert to teach us—yes, us, we live here, too— then we have a responsibility to the town, to the community, to help, to educate.

The classroom set up of SWT/110: Staring at Walls
and Thinking While Seated was remarkably similar to any
other course one would have taken. We did not experiment with the form or presentation of the class. Certain
traditional elements were yet present in those first mild
experiments. There was a classroom. Rows of desks. A
chalkboard. An instructor, who paced back and forth,
sometimes making notes on the board, sometimes sitting
at a desk, sometimes struggling with a DVD player and
television on top of a rolling stand. Students doodled
in margins. The class met in the school's main building.
There was a bell. The only unique ingredient, then, was
the content. There was a growing demand for less academic and more useful offerings. The students were as-
signed an hour of staring at a wall in their home offices,
then their dining rooms, then their bedrooms. In class,
groups of students would observe ten to fifteen minutes of
one another staring at the wall with the chalkboard, then
the opposing wall with affixed pencil sharpener to com-
pare and contrast differing results. Our critics chuckled
to themselves, figuring we'd go by the wayside. But after
Staring at Walls and Thinking While Seated, we created
more New Practicals: Looking in the Mirror While Depressed; Developing Personal Superstition to Provide Irrational Hope and Dread; Walking Aimlessly in Known
Locations; Improper Memories of the Dead; Novel Reading Without Paying Attention. All of these courses remained in the schoolhouse. We heard some ponder aloud:
"Is this really school? Are these legitimate 'classes'?" But
many accepted the offerings, showing up to the institution's building for particular classes that met at particular times with particular expectations.

It is not our mission to "take over" the town, as some in the media have suggested. Our mission, as we stated from the beginning, which everyone at first appreciated, was, has always been, is, and will continue to be to educate the citizens of this fine community, of which we are fiercely loyal members. We are proud educators. If our practices have changed, if our offerings have deviated from "the norm," this is in no way intended to harm anyone or the community as a whole. To the contrary: we aim to educate and help, yes, help everyone in this town. Some critics have decided that we are now aiming toward a revolution, but we are humble. Revolution has never been our pursuit. We love where we live and would change not one thing about it. We simply wish to offer, to those who desire it, the best education we can provide in whatever field they choose. It is not "radical" to create curricula suited for the chosen ambitions of so many of our citizens. If we were harming individuals, then we would see a drop in enrollment. However, we see only demand and gratitude. It may sound as if we are defending ourselves, and to some extent we are, and to some extent we are resentful at having to do so. And although we refuse to apologize for creating just what we have a need for, the staff, board, faculty, and loyal students of the Community School feel pressured to clear their names. We never thought anyone would label what we do "increasingly dangerous." Our critics claimed that there was nothing to learn from our courses. They claimed to not need these lessons. They believed that they were all fine, believed themselves to be *well*, believed they had nothing to learn. Our opposition leveled accusations that Our New Community School was creating a new "class" of dissatisfied people. Honest people. But we are proud of our brave students. We will not go away, as some clearly want from us. We will not hang our heads. But we will, also, not pretend to be unaware of the vicious opinions that are circulating.

Form

There is a difference between who we are on the inside of this wall and who we are when we walk out the sliding glass doors of the main entrance, to the other side, to the sidewalks. Within these walls, we are a dedicated and passionate group of educators and students. On the other side, we are people living lives, having successes and failures, squeezing avocados at the market, all on our own, without a mentor. But this division was an impediment to some courses. We have a policy at the Community School of allowing any individual associated with the endeavor, from board member to night security guard, to make suggestions that improve our level of education. One such suggestion from our web manager, Keith, for a New New Practical in Achieving Geographical Disorientation in the Modern World, we believed to be a breakthrough, the kind of idea that seemed so incisive that we were shocked not to have thought it before. Keith requested to teach a course outside the main campus. He noted that wisdom could be imparted in the classroom, but many of his insights came to him in the alleys of our town, out in the park, in the sunlight, or during a rainstorm. If he could have students meet in the park, where they could, for the allotted time, wander and disorient in a natural environment, the students' appreciation and advancement would accelerate. We sought real-world application of our most important subjects, a chance for students to learn not only the academic but the applicable. To do so, we ventured out of the classroom. After content, we experimented with form. It didn't make sense, in most cases, to meet in a white-walled classroom with desks and air conditioning units and fluorescent lights humming. The very essence of a New Practical course is to prepare students for the intellectual lives they will someday lead. And almost nothing is applicable in a classroom on the third floor of a schoolhouse. The classroom is a vacuum, a space where information flows most easily and the actual application of information proves impossible. We reassigned our Encountering Scents to Conjure Unidentified Nostalgia class to meet at scheduled class times in gardens and kitchens around town; our Feeling Small in the Scope of History course to meet amid the ruins of centuries-old forts and barracks; our Cultivating Irrational Fear class to meet at the hospital; our Observing Art While Lamenting Why God Did Not Bestow Upon Us Talent class to meet in museums and galleries; our Acute Regretting of the Cheap and Ruinous Affair courses in bars and cafés and motel rooms. Students initially showed up to the forests and museums of our town with their backpacks and satchels, looking for numbers on doors. They were stressed when finding the meeting places, often asking museum patrons if they had seen a group of students. But eventually, the students settled. They reluctantly gave up their notebooks and pens, their books and desks. They eased into it. The instructors were patient, allowing students several more minutes to arrive than they usually would in the classroom setting. Over time, everyone realized that learning did not happen solely in the classroom, that education could be refreshed, that meaning could come through in more and more environments, in these new forms. We razed all buildings on campus but the main schoolhouse. Our very first traditional courses—the poetry, the computer science, the history—with their dwindling student numbers, continued to meet in white-walled classrooms with a window slightly cracked, letting a sliver of the outside in.

Structure

Empowerment and confidence are the most useful things to gain from a course. If a student feels comfortable with his or her own ideas, confident that he or she can contribute to a field of study—whether it is another institution's traditional offering of British Romantic Poetry or our New New Practical of Picking a Daisy While Feeling Ugly—then the course has succeeded in bestowing upon the student all it can hope to. The role of teacher and student will always imply a disparity in authority, in command of subject. Instructors observed that students continually deferred to them. And so, many instructors took to disguising themselves in the New New Classroom. The teacher would not lecture in the galleries and restaurants and subway stations. Instead, an instructor would arrive and pretend to be meeting with the group like any other student. When no instruction came, when no one announced him or herself as the leader of the class, the groups panicked and sometimes dissolved. There were no syllabi. We didn't anticipate the level of anxiety caused by the lack of syllabi. Many students reported the need for a clearer set of expectations. Many students walked out of New New Classes. But those students who continued to attend the classes that met in the park, on benches, under oak trees to learn to Talk About the Weather and

Look Down to Hide a Reddening Face and Welling Tears with more ease, those who stuck it out reported learning "actual tools." And this is when we saw critics suggest that we were misleading our students, pulling the wool over their eyes, insulting the educational system itself, rebelling. They said we shouldn't delude our students into thinking that these careers were within reach.

Over time, students became comfortable with no identifiable instructor. They taught themselves, confident that an expert was among the group and guiding the lesson unnoticed. Groups of students gathered at the bar to Remember Childhood Dreams and Eye Strangers With Growing Envy. They realized that they had more learning to do; they could learn from each other, be experts themselves. The instructors, too, noted a refreshing take on subjects they had previously taken to be their forte. Instructors learned. Students taught. Walking in the woods, groups of people asked each other if anyone knew How to Return Home to Apologize Too Late; riding on buses, students looked out the window to View Passing Row Homes of Impoverished Neighborhoods and Feel Unjustified for Personal Sadness. And when class ended, they headed home to share what they had learned.

Time Frame

As if we were the arbiters of education, we, the Community School, were blind to the idea that learning could occur outside class start and class end. Many in town believed that we had vanished when the brochures ceased to be printed, when our website disappeared, when we no longer listed the courses that met outside the crumbling

schoolhouse. Time was our final experiment. Now, every
moment became teachable. Randomly, while playing tennis
in the park, a person may, all of a sudden, Acknowledge
Loss of Youth. All of a sudden, in line at the post office,
a person may reveal him- or herself to be a teacher while
Gripping a Long Overdo Love Letter to be Finally Sent.
Buying milk and eggs can be done with deeper Distrac-
tion from Lost Ambition. Discussing a television show
with a spouse can alloy with Resignation for a Life With
the Wrong Person. Our classes happened spontaneously.
Washing a mug from a zoo in California, right then,
something educational about Realizing It Is Too Late to
Take the Risk. Checking the mailbox and never seeing
the letter in order to Confirm the Missed Opportunity.
Sipping coffee can become a significant moment of Foolish Thoughts Over Legacy. One-on-one courses of one,
two, three seconds in length. Examining one's job benefits portfolio, quickly, a single person, teacher and student combined, squints through her reading glasses and
calls class to attention in her mind, lecturing silently on
the subject of Replacing Hope with Responsibility. We
will not go away. We cannot stop. We want to help you.
We want to be helped.

Sometimes, a member of the community will pop in at the
old schoolhouse, where we began our pursuit to educate.
Sometimes, people sign up for a foreign language course.
And while reciting the declensions of a particular verb,
students and teacher alike will look out that cracked-
open window and believe this is the only way, the proper
way to learn.

Camp Redo

I'm going for the pussy badge. It's my last one left. I got the midnight-rendezvous-by-tire-swing-over-water badge; the getting-caught-running-through-girls'-cabin-with-underwear-on-head; the sneak-a-beer-on-roof-of-mess-hall. All I need is the pussy badge. And you know what? I'm going to get it.

We are allowed personal calls on Sundays. Mostly I call Steven to check in on the restaurant, and my wife to get an update on the kids. When I call, I talk like a thirteen-year-old (required for the "full experience"). I say: "Hey, Susie, how's it going? (Then I pause like I don't care), and then say: "Yeah, yeah, I love you, too, Sue. Gotta run." And then I hang up the phone and run to hang out with my new best friends on the dock. When I run, I run like a thirteen-year-old over to the pond (legs flailing out at the sides, almost a skip). I was taught in orientation to jump from time to time for no particular reason, like the spontaneity of being a new teen. I got the running-like-a-carefree-kid badge real early on here.

At the dock, they're all wearing swim trunks circa late '80s, and the girls (women) have their hair in that era's style, too. Scooter (Dr. Phillips) hasn't done well in completing badge missions, so he's still working on push-new-best-friend-into-water badge. Me, I've got my eyes on Betsy (Professor Stevenson from the small college in the city). She's going to give me my pussy badge, and I'm going to give her her penis badge. I shove her in the water, tell her she's an idiot, and then ask her to meet me back here after lights out. She giggles and says, "Eww gross," and, "No way." I know she'll be there.

It's a catch-22, in a way. When you get all the badges, you're done. So, you can't stay. But until you get all the badges, you haven't fulfilled your lost childhood. So, you see? I have mixed feelings as I skip whimsically (for the full experience) in the shadows down to the water. I know that I have to get the pussy badge, and Betsy needs the penis, but then it will all be over.

I remove my sandals and throw away my gum and dip my feet, up to my knees, in the cool pond water, making ripples in the moon's line of white on the black satin. Luckily, no one is around when I break character and remove my oversized baseball cap and rub my bald head. I catch myself and put the oversized cap back on (askew of course). My camp-issued T-shirt, bearing the logo of my favorite sports team (a team I've never heard of) hangs over my nylon shorts, covering my gut (supposedly making me look like a fat kid, not an overweight restaurant manager). I wait, trying to think about capture-the-flag and shaving cream on my best friends' hands, and warm water to make them piss—but I keep thinking about where I will go tomorrow, after I get Betsy's pussy badge. Sue, the kids, my job, bills, all the dreams I gave up. And the thought of a wife, kids, a job (my wife, my kids, my job), it hurts. So, I continue to think about batting for the baseball team on my shirt, hitting home runs and playing for the rest of my life, having wishes. I think about building giant Lincoln Log cabins, snow forts, tree houses, and living in them with my best friends forever and ever. I skip a stone, picture ladybugs, and sharply dream of catching fireflies, blocking it all out for just one more night. Then, I hear someone step onto the dock behind me.

She doesn't say a word. She won't meet my eyes, awkward, looking all around, glancing behind her, appearing nervous about getting caught (she's good at this). I try to try looking cool (in the frame of mind of a thirteen-year-old) and don't say anything either. Betsy sits down next to me, leaving a foot of space on the dock in between our wrinkled bodies and youthful personas. She knows it, and I know it: I'm getting in her pants, and she's getting into mine. But I don't want to leave this camp. I want to fail this mission. But I can't tell if she does.

"You got some gum?" I ask, looking at the water.

"Yeah, here you go." She reaches into her pocket and pulls out nothing, mimes removing gum from a pack, then hands it to me (she's really good).

"Thanks."

"No problem." She laughs a little, then sighs and swings her legs, skimming the top of the black pond with her toes. I like the look of her thigh all of a sudden and reach around her waist and kiss her on the mouth, pull back, remove the gum, throw it, and then push my hand up her shirt and feel my face heat up. She takes her shirt off, and I am awed. I've never seen boobs before. I reach down her frayed jean shorts, undoing the button and pulling on the zipper. This is so new, so scary. What is down there, under her shorts? How will it feel? What should I do? Then I touch it—it feels so unclear—and before I even realize that I have finally graduated, I remove the badge from her shorts. I lean back, catching my breath, allowing her to pull down my nylon shorts. She reaches down and removes the penis badge, and we hug. We sit there, still, a little proud, a little foolish. We realize we have to leave this place, and we hug. Hug and cry, and get scared for the future.

A Proper Hunger

Although we had all seen the bubbling tanks with rubber-banded and sullen lobsters at the front of the house in many restaurants—displayed to assure the patron that the crustaceans would be fresh killed and were living, however pitifully, mere moments before being consumed, producing the effect of allowing the wild outside world into the ordered environs of the eating establishment, and adding, too, a reminder of where food comes from, providing higher consciousness to the meal, building layers of understanding and perhaps respect, but mostly displayed there for us diners to feel confident ordering lobster at the restaurant because it wouldn't taste funny (for no one who has eaten a non-fresh lobster can forget the weirdness of the mouthful, the unpleasantness of the realization, the minor horror of the experience)—and though we had recently learned of the locavore movement in certain areas in the Northeast and the West Coast—eateries intent on minimizing the distance foods travel from ground, wilderness, sky, or sea to kitchen, maintaining a guarantee of peak freshness, allowing for fewer if any preservatives to be injected into the ingredients, ensuring that the foods are in season, restricting the patron for the patron's sake, limiting the menu to foods that would be available to a wild man, perhaps an early pilgrim, all of which philosophies brought forth in us the revelation that we hadn't been eating as we should eat, that we had, somewhere along the line, been duped by some great unknown food charlatan, assuring us that this meal was good, correct, safe, proper, natural, organic, celebratory, rare, our new favorite, gave us a new "vore" suffix, which we liked very much, and had us telling everyone about new farm-to-table restaurants that others must try, because it was the ideal way to eat— and although, finally, we had all, of course, dabbled (with varying degrees of success) in Community Sponsored Agricultures and home gardening and public gardening—plots wherein we planted our tomato vines and basil plants and pepper seeds and cabbage roots, where we dug our fingers into the soil, smiled up into the sun and prayed for the suckers to grow and yield, and which sometimes did grow and yield, and which we did pluck and carry to our home kitchens to make salad or pasta sauce or stew, a fact that delighted us and our guests to no end ("you grew this? you plucked it this afternoon?") and was ultimately a stronger connection to our meals, carrying, as it did, notes of self-sufficiency and patience and wonderment at ingredients that were mere dirt weeks ago—despite all this, we were unprepared for the next steps in dining.

As much as we had thought we had connected with our food, acknowledged where it came from, thought about it as not simply a filet mignon on our plate but a cut from the short loin of an actual sentient living steer, we realized we were fooling ourselves with how connected we thought ourselves when Animal Farm, the first of the "New Restaurants," showcased its livestock, in a larger-scale version of the lobster tank, in a covered barn attached to the restaurant. A long glass window gave sight of the cows, pigs, chickens, lambs, turkeys, and ducks, housed in this hay-floored room, as patrons walked in the front

door. Along the wall, above the lobster tank, the long
window proved to us that everything was fresh. There
they were. Walking around. The animals were treated
very well. Cage free. No antibiotics. No hormones. The
animals looked happy enough in that room, through the
long window, as we entered. Happier than the pitiful lobsters awaiting their hot fates. The closest farm-to-table
experience one could get.

Some of us found this unnerving for various reasons.
Some thought the barnyard "right there!" was unsani-
tary. The animals coming directly from the barn into the
kitchen could trail disease or "something gross." Others
were unsettled to lock eyes with a huge mammal or adorable fowl for which they were hungering. They couldn't
bring themselves to order the T-bone now. But some did
anyway, mostly at the urging of their tablemates and the
convincing arguments thrown about by fellow patrons
and the restaurant management itself.

"I can't order the execution of that living animal."

"You do it all the time when you order bacon or ribs."

"But that animal's already dead."

"No, you just don't see it. You must remember where
your food comes from."

"I know. It's just hard."

"You would rather a thousand anonymous animals
packed into steel cages be slaughtered en masse, butchered and shipped thousands of miles in a freight hold?"

"No."

"But you're saying that's easier."

"It is."

"You know nothing. Order your pork belly. Think
about it. Connect with it. Don't be a hypocrite. Don't be
ignorant."

Our obsession was not entirely for the health benefits or in spite of the inconvenience, though, of course, these reasons were apparent and bandied about and debated (for the food was less sterile, the potential contact with disease was greater, the likelihood of waiting an extra 45 minutes for the preparation—which we did not complain about—was increased), but instead for the imbued spiritual connection with the act of eating, the regression in the progression. We had come too far in culinary arts and genetic modifications; it was for the communion with food, the return to the earthly things we had forgotten to recall.

The restaurant, undoubtedly predicting this unnerving sensation, had taken great pains to dazzle the patron once at her table. After viewing the barnyard through the long window, you wouldn't believe such a room was adjacent to the one in which you ate. The copper-topped tables adorned with pressed, white linen napkins, rolled to contain spotless silverware that clanged and sparkled upon revelation, the gleaming white side dishes and solid square bottles of olive oil, the adorable ribbed ramekins containing pats of butter, with equally cute butter knives laid askew, the ambient music slipping from speakers hidden within brick walls or behind fish tanks, everything harmonizing, presentations of wine bottles, standing stainless steel ice buckets, holding champagne at sixty-degree angles, thin glass flutes ready for the most delicate of clinking, bowing servers clad in black, menus perfumed with lavender, and a dimming of the lights at the proper dining hour. Everything sophisticated, as one would expect of a place with $90 entrées. To further draw attention away from the rawness of the barn-room, Animal Farm served a perfect mis-en-scène on dishes. Green leaves in the left-hand corner of the white plate. Towering blackened meat, cut to impossibly straight right angles on all sides with orange sauce hypnotically swirled on top, but with the edge dotted for the sake of the composition. Edible flower petals of purple and white flanking each meal. We often commented that we didn't want to ruin the artwork by consuming it. But ruin the artwork, we did. We left our forks and knives crossed in perfect X's on our finished plates. We touched the corners of our mouths with linen and left the napkins crumpled next to our plates, an imperfect accent to highlight the perfection. Then, a clean table, and an ordering of espresso. Black liquid holes within porcelain. Delicate finger tips. Pinkies extended. Gracious. Our experiences began when we arrived early for a drink at the bar, after passing the long window into the barn-room. Civilized, we thought. And our experiences ended with a black leather-bound book. A white slip of slick and curling paper. A plastic sleeve. A passing. An autograph. We dined in the city. Then, arm in arm, we strolled out into the brisk night. We were conscious, connected, satisfied, and in need of nothing else but rest.

But there was yet a gap between our meals and the stock from which it was prepared, from which it was slaughtered and butchered. Slaughterhouse-Five, the newest of the "New Restaurants" was set up much the same way as Animal Farm, with one important difference: Whatever one ordered, one killed for his or her own meal. It was the first of the "kill-and-eat" chic restaurants. When one ordered a half roast chicken, one was escorted by a server, wearing a heavy apron and rubber boots, to the barn-room and there selected a chicken, a similar but invariably new experience to the old-hat ritual with the lobster. After selection, the chicken was moved into a special slaughter room, and the patron was handed a butcher knife. A staff member placed the chicken's head between two nails on a long dark block, steadied the bird. The patron raised the blade and struck down, severing head from body. This brought on tears in some cases. To take a life in such a direct manner is an experience that shocks and sticks. Anyone who has boiled a lobster and spoken to the crustacean before dropping it into the bubbling bath knows that this act is not the same as swatting a mosquito. Inevitably, however, it is somehow more humane, because the departed is to be eaten, not simply flicked off a forearm onto the lawn. Those who ordered hamburgers pressed the button to send a bolt through the cranium of the cow they had chosen. Rabbits were struck repeatedly in the head with a short heavy rod until limp. This provided a dining experience like no other: the table conversation, and the true connection to the process of slaughtering the meal to be eaten. The chicken had never tasted so special. The burger never had more meaning.

"This is no longer a mystery. I have looked into the lamb's eyes. I have chosen it. I have killed it consciously. And I am eating it. One does this all the time without knowing it, and now I am fully aware."

Vegetarians, on the other hand, took a pleasant trip to the restaurant's garden with a server to pluck leaves, tomatoes, cucumbers, grains, and mushrooms. It seemed the experience of "kill-and-eat" forced would-be carnivores into vegetarianism. Men and women came to terms with their previous willing ignorance, grew now completely sure that they could not kill to eat.

The contrast between hay-strewn barn-room and elegant dining area was next to go. Instead of a long window giving sight of the animals, patrons entered a vestibule that opened into the barn-room, through which they walked before entering a dining room that had seen all the frills removed. Gone were the gleaming plates and sparkling silverware, the too-white linen and champagne flutes and porcelain ramekins. Gone were the fish tanks and ambient music, the lights on dimmers, the two-tops and four-tops of copper plated tables. Gone were the servers in black, even the black aprons and black boots. Now the servers donned coveralls, wore kerchiefs in their hair, dried blood on their denim. The dining room at Pilgrim's Progress was composed of long communal tables, warped and beaten wood tops, where one sat among strangers for a shared experience. Suddenly it seemed ridiculous to have previously separated oneself from the other diners by an arbitrary distance between tables. The once common rule of sitting with your party and ostensibly ignoring the fact that there were others eating near you had vanished. It was a thing of our past, a custom of other less tactful people at other less sophisticated restaurants to be upset at overhearing conversations at nearby tables. Now, we introduced ourselves to those around us. We all talked of the experience. And, indeed, the experience of eating the meal became more ceremonious when shared with strangers who became new friends. We offered bites of the turkey we had slain. They made up side plates of rabbit for us to try. We all had something to chat about, of course, so it wasn't as awkward as we imagined it would be. We always discussed the changes in dining.

"It's funny how you become so used to change. How quickly the past seems silly. How much more enjoyable eating is when you are more a part of the entire process. To see the animals, the gardens. To take the action to kill what will be your meal. I feel so foolish for never having even inquired as to where the ingredients came from before."

"Well, I still don't like it very much. I don't eat meat, and I hate that I still have to look at the poor animals who should be free."

"But they are treated far better, and you can plainly see as much. God knows what was happening to them before."

"I feel a great connection to the meals now. I don't eat meat unless I am able to see it for myself first. This has made me a more educated, considerate, sensitive eater. You can't deny that your wish for animals to not be eaten is, in part, aided by these establishments. Many people have refused and come face to face with their previous ignorance, you see."

"But it's still just a masking of the facts. We are still raising animals for livestock. We are still holding them captive. We are still denying them animal-lives."

Perhaps someone had the same conversation in another "kill-and-eat" restaurant, or perhaps someone near this precise conversation at Pilgrim's Progress was integral to the next step in dining. To further obliterate the hierarchy of man over beast and seeming brutality of holding animals hostage, as it were, WILD!, a new restaurant at the far edge of the city, near the great West Forest, boasted a menu that did not contain merely cage-free, free-range, organic, natural, and "kill-and-eat" steaks, lamb chops, and pork loin. This new restaurant promised that all meals would be entirely "free."

The great West Forest is a peninsula, a sort of large and natural pen, jutting into the Moshpee Lake. Once patrons arrived through the vestibule, there was no long window and no barn-room to pass through before entering a rustic dining hall; there was a prep room.

We were outfitted with binoculars and canteens and duck whistles, and, most incredibly, weapons of our choosing. Cross-bow. Rifle. Bowie knife. Trap. Machete. The restaurant, however, maintained a strict black-tie dress code. Wild, yes, but civilized through and through.

A personal account is in order here, as I won't soon forget my first trip out into the woods with my party. Our wives hesitated, so we told them that we fellas would go, check it out, have a guys' night to try out the new restaurant. We arrived in our black tuxes and black bow ties, and just as promised, we were presented with our choice of weapons (we chose the net, the machete, the crossbow, and the rifle). In our formal wear with our paraphernalia, we sidled up to the bar for an aperitif. A few cocktails before the meal. We had arrived, as advised by WILD!, an hour before seating time, to hunt our meals. The cocktails were fantastic. We were all smiles, holding up our weapons and saying, "Can you believe this! It's outstanding!" and posing for pictures. But then our server—acting as a guide, dressed in a white shirt with black tie, and apron, linen napkin draped over his forearm—tapped us on the shoulder and signaled that we should head out now. He took our glasses and carried them on a silver platter into the woods.

The three of us friends, to my knowledge, had never hunted, barely fished. The most "wild" we had been was in Pilgrim's Progress and Slaughterhouse-Five, where we were allowed to simply kill the animals, while their breeding, feeding, raising, and holding were all executed by the restaurant staff, the farmhands, as they were. Now, we had no one handing us a bolt gun while the steer calmly knelt in a harness, no nails to hold the turkey's head while we made one quick drop of the knife, no server tying up the rabbit for bashing. We were in nature. We weren't in a shifty verisimilitude of farm life, which was how we now viewed those previous restaurants. We were in it—perhaps of it.

We sneaked along behind the server, who was all the while very serious, very rigid in his posture, carrying the platter of drinks, extending it out to us when we took breaks throughout the trek. He marched with his chin up, confident and calm. He did not speak. Instead, with his free arm, keeping the linen napkin draped just so, he flashed hand signals, which were surprisingly clear, though foreign to us. A splayed hand straight up—stop. A ticking pointer finger to the east—go. A lowered closed hand—crouch, wait. Two fingers that at first resembled a peace sign but then pointed—look, see, target.

    I followed his horizontal peace sign through the trees out into a clearing. We were at the tree line before an expanse of green that ran up to a cliff, beyond which was the lake. I felt good. I saw this scene. It was beautiful to be in it, a part of it, really. So far removed from the hustle and bustle. It was genuine—that's the word. I unfastened the top button of my dress shirt.

    But then my eyes fell on what the server intended for me to find out there. A buck. It was chewing the grass of the small plain. Its mouth a mess of black gums and green mush. That rocking jaw. The chewing. The horns. Pale yellow horns like oak branches in winter reaching sharp points. The smooth, muscular brown sheen of coarse hair. Clouds letting go the sun. The deer twitching its ears to swat a fly. Big brown eyes. The animal was gorgeous in this free wilderness. In this wild. It was right.

The server, calm and confident, chin up, back to a tree, signaled for me to wait. I, in turn, signaled the target to the two in my party, who readied their weapons. I signaled to wait. Patience.

The deer turned away from the tree line and showed us its hind quarters. This is what the server was asking us to wait for. This opportunity to sneak up on the prey. He signaled for me to go—use the net.

My first thought was that I was going to get trampled. Impaled. I was going to botch this kill. I would spook the animal and it would charge me, mess of horns pointed at my heart. I wouldn't be agile in my polished shoes. But I remembered my weapons, and perhaps if it did go badly, I could throw the net, trip it up, confuse it, distract it, while I escaped and the server assisted me to safety. My next thought: *this is, after all, a business, a restaurant.* It is not entirely real. It is all orchestrated to some degree, controlled. They will not let me die. If not for the humanity of it, for the lawsuit. I took a breath and raised myself up. I signaled for my party to follow in after me. Slow. Quiet. It would be my kill this time.

I crept through the trees and stepped into the light of the small plain. Ducks flew overhead, toward the lake. I spied a turkey by the tree line at my nine o'clock, but I wanted venison today. I focused on the deer, still facing out away from me to the cliff. It was twenty yards away at most.

Then the deer turned, and I instinctively rotated with it to keep myself hidden behind the beast. It stopped and put its head down for more leaves.

I charged.

It raised its head at my footfall. Then it sprang, darting away. I heaved the net, which flew fast and spread like

a parachute, weighted at six points. The trap landed over
the animal. It reared up, which entangled it further. Its
hooves were now stuck through the mesh. Its horns were
pinned down in the enclosing web. It was tying itself in
a tighter and tighter ball of netting. The deer rocked up
and down, spinning in circles. I watched, heart racing. I
had actually done it. I had actually done it. This would
be my kill.

In a final show of its incredible strength and will,
the snared beast roared and bucked, airborne. The netting ripped at the horns. I thought, *they won't let me die.*
Then I remembered signing contracts in triplicate before
cocktails. Waivers. Did I read them? The deer thrashed its
beautiful head and horns on its strong neck. Its shoulders
rippled and flexed. Its legs kicked like whips. The mesh
tore, and the buck's head came free.

I looked to the tree line, for the server, for my party.
They remained crouched near the edge of the plain.

The server was signaling madly. He was waving the
linen napkin. He was chopping with his arm, dropping
the platter. Chopping and chopping.

I returned to the animal, which was now calm and
facing me. It snorted. The mess of black gums and green
mush now bloody. It lowered its head, pointed its horns,
and charged. But the netting at its legs caught, and it collapsed in a thunderous heap not two feet from where I
stood frozen.

I heard the server, doing away with signals, just holler-
ing: "Slit its throat! Cut its throat! Now! Cut its throat!"

I reached to my side for the machete and withdrew
the weapon from the sheath. A long, wide steel menace
with weight. I raised it above the head of the snared buck
and—when it swung its head back, exposing its smooth

brown-and-white tender neck—I brought down the blade.

Its head had jerked down quickly, and the machete met with its snout, chopping off a quarter of its black nose and a part of its top lip. Blood spurted. The animal made a sound like a gurgling bleat. I swung again and the blade stuck in its throat. I backed off, as it thrashed a moment more, then calmed and finally bled out.

After the server helped us quarter and cart away the meat, we slumped at our communal table under a great blue tent on the grass of the patio area, near men in tuxedos and women in shimmering dresses. Other patrons, in blood-splattered dress shirts, equally exhausted by the ritual, ordered liquor and beer in a few hushed syllables, awaiting their dinner as the sun set. There wasn't much conversation. Some examined their weapons and smiled dimly when we met their eyes.

The venison arrived, and we grabbed at it with our hands, ripping the meat with our teeth. But we swallowed as quickly as we could. It was only hunger. We paid the bill and shouldered the bags of raw meat from our kill. We separated and somehow wandered home.

Even as "Wild Restaurants," as they were known, became the rage, even as we hurled ourselves passionately into the new style of dining, we felt a secret resistance, a desire for something else. Did we crave a restaurant in which we had to kill animals with our bare hands? Did we crave raw flesh? Did we desire more of a challenge? A three-day fast before the dining hour? Did we want to eat worms and spiders and beetles? Whatever it might be, whatever form this desire took, we felt a need for it rising up from deep within.

It was in this atmosphere of passion and secret dissat-isfaction that we heard of a new restaurant. As with most novel ideas, the first of the "Future Restaurants" had taken a common assumption in the current climate of dining and subverted it The Laboratory, as it was called, was a rebuke of the natural, organic, rural, rustic, archaic, and earth-infested establishments. The restaurant provided a truly new way to dine. They offered similar menus to those of Pilgrim's and Animal Farm and Slaughterhouse, with one important exception: all meat dishes were "never-live."

After the vestibule, we entered and saw, again, a long window that showed a white room, with lab-coated men and women in goggles, holding up vials, leaning over mi-croscopes, and pulling stainless steel trays of quivering mounds of muscle and fat and bone from under glass labo-ratory hoods. One could identify almost immediately, the lump of yellowish protein as chicken, or mound of bleeding red tissue as beef, the tender pink strips of flesh as rab-bit. But other ingredients were entirely unrecognizable. These "meats" were grown on white protein scaffolds of loin, liver, stomach, wing, and heart, the menu explained. The muscle and fat concoctions were then shuttled into the kitchen on conveyor belts. It was a tight ship. A good clean process.

The dining room was a welcomed return to elegance, with kitsch accents like beakers for champagne flutes, gauze for napkins, clamps and scalpels for silverware. The kitchen staff and servers wore hospital scrubs, and the dinners were served on stainless steel and sectioned rect-angular plates. Some meals came with capsules as sides, pills of yellow and pink. The plates of meat glowed red, shaped into small pyramids or perfect circles. The salad leaves were squares. Some meats were transparent.

The taste was similar to meals of our past, meals of real living things. Not exact, if only for its superiority. There was no variety in the quality of the animal, no chance of putting two duck breasts in the oven and discovering one slightly more cooked than the other.

Conversation ramped up again. The purity of eating everything one could want and without the need of breeding and holding an animal or stalking and murdering. This was the solution. And the connection to the food, the communion with the dining experience was altogether fresh. It was as if we were eating in the way the progress of humanity would someday take us, should someday take us; we were on a path to this way of eating already throughout civilization. Everything was controlled—no fear of E. coli or mad cow disease or some new mutation in the livestock. Even the cholesterol and fat content could be predetermined at each batch. This was how it would be, and we were the lucky few to have it now.

After inhaling lab-generated espressos through vaporizers and autographing sizable checks, we, once again, strolled into the crisp night, satisfied. We once again enjoyed making our reservations and showing up to the bar for aperitifs and getting into long dresses and sport coats. The meals were ours again. And really truly ours, as scientific creatures on this earth, among beasts.

Of course, though, we all knew there would be another new restaurant, already in the works perhaps, that would come along and show us how we were wrong before, we were wrong now. We would gladly try it out. We knew that. But until then, we were confident we had made it.

But other times we will be sitting in the park on a warm Sunday afternoon, reading a book, not yet thinking of dinner. Totally content. And then our stomach will growl. We will feel a twist on our insides, a biological dis-comfort. Hunger. And we will do just about anything to make it go away.

3.
WITNESS MAGICAL THINGS!

Porcelain God

The dudes who remodeled my mom's master bathroom plumb forgot to take away the old pink toilet. So, there it stood, in the middle of our front yard—a constant amidst the turning, falling leaves of autumn.

We figured they'd be back for it, the toilet. After a week or so of rousing suspicion among the other residents of Green Street though, the unspoken realization hit us: that pink throne was our problem now.

One crisp November afternoon, my mom and brother and I all found ourselves standing around the thing with steaming cups of coffee in our hands. My mug had a chip and read "Nobody's Perfect."

"How heavy is it?" My brother tried his best to surmise the toilet's heft with his mind then tilted it with his free hand.

"Don't hurt yourself," cautioned my mother.

"Well?" I wanted to hear that it was no problem; that Simon would throw it on his back and carry it to wherever hoppers go to rest in peace.

"Like a boulder," he said, sliding a timid step back from it, sipping his coffee.

We just stared at the thing for a while, in silence. A leaf landed on it. We eyed each other.

Later on, we were back in separate rooms of the house, all of us pretty sure that that toilet situation would just take care of itself.

———

If my dad hadn't gone and had a heart attack and died during a tennis date last winter, we would have let him deal with the throne's removal. It was his after all. Well, we all conducted business with it, over the years, the taco nights. But my dad, he used it exclusively, never settling for a leak in the downstairs half bath, or maybe just a gassy false alarm in the upstairs hall john. The rest of us were equal opportunity with our ones and twos.

The only time I saw my father naked, he was draining the lizard into that pink toilet. He was upset, I remember. I was little; I flung open the door and froze. My old man looked up; he sighed; he breathed my name. He was never angry before or after that. Something cosmic transpired between my dad and the pink toilet that my encroaching upon disrupted. Also, outside that moment, I never saw him vulnerable. But, of course, he was vulnerable and probably pretty pissed when his heart went and dropped the ball at deuce point.

———

Besides the toilet on the lawn, there were other new features at the Clark household. For one, my brother was there all the time. He bailed on his life across the country, in San Francisco, after Dad bailed on his for good. When December rolled around, Simon began to pick up the pieces, got a marketing gig in Beantown, started saving for an apartment. I was in my senior year at a ridiculous private school, applying to ridiculous colleges. California schools looked good junior year, but I narrowed the list to campuses within driving distance of our house, closer to our pink toilet. Mom, despite talking vaguely of renewing her RN credits, stayed locked away in her room more and more. When I returned from school, she would be wrapped in her red and black flannel robe, in bed watching bad Lifetime movies, or at the computer googling involved French recipes that I certainly never had the pleasure of eating.

We were curious when the first snowfall began covering the pink toilet—would the thing go out of sight, out of mind? Early one morning, the first flakes made a white and pink polka-dotted sculpture of the toilet in our yard.

"Shit," shouted my brother, and I hadn't sensed that he was standing behind me, watching through the window, too. "We need to take a picture." He ran off, then appeared in the yard with his camera, motioning for me to come out, and mouthing "bring the paper." I grabbed the Sunday *Globe* and trotted down the steps.

We met up at the toilet.

"Sit on it," he said.

"On the toilet?"

"Like you're taking a shit."

I lifted the seat.

"Don't actually crap in the thing. Just sit on the lid."

I did so.

"Now read the paper." Simon danced around and snapped photos from all angles. At first, he was framing the shots for like whole minutes, preserving the moment, the image, me on the toilet. He looked so focused, like he was staring at a developing cure in a petri dish. All of a sudden, I wanted to try and deal with it like my brother; I got into the whole charade. I mimed unzipping and fire hosing it. I pretended to barf, praying to the porcelain God. I laughed. My bro laughed. I faked all embarrassed like getting barged in on. Posing for a swirly proved too difficult. When we were through, Simon out of film, I depressed the handle, folded the paper under my arm, and whistled my way back inside with Simon chuckling and winding his camera behind me.

At the new toilet, relieving myself of what all the pretend bathroom business had conjured, I thought, so that's how it happens, that's how people wind up with junk on display around their property: something is kind of too heavy or annoying to remove, then you get attached to it. It was sad and scary that my dad was a doctor, I was in private school. But none of that matters when you've got a toilet in your front yard—Presto—White Trash.

It was a white Christmas that year, first in a decade we were told. Mom said we were too grown-up to get presents, to get a tree, to put up the little white lights, and we agreed. I didn't want any gifts anyhow, at least nothing that she could have given me. We gave Mom a nosegay of daisies and yellow roses though, and, of course, she cried, and Christmas was saved only when Simon rolled up an eternally constipated snowman to sit on the snowtoilet. He called Mom out to see, and she laughed. When she laughed, it was good. I watched through the window, her breath a misty cloud, then gone. The snowman strained. It was good for her and for Simon.

After New Year's, a new orange bottle fluttered into existence on the white laminate countertop of our kitchen. Mom called them her happy pills. She didn't seem to be taking the proper amount at first. It is slightly more upsetting, I noticed, to have someone around who is too happy rather than too sad when you know it's just manufactured smiles. Either way, throughout that winter, Mom was out of bed before me, with breakfast made and everything.

"Am I doing an okay job with you, sweetie?" she asked, over scrambled eggs and coffee.

"Of course, Mom. You're the best." I didn't look up.

"Good. I'm so proud of you, you know."

"I know."

"Dad is proud of you, too."

Pregnant pause.

"You can talk to him, you know." She brushed my hair back with the tips of her fingers. My head, a block of ice.

Along with my mother's newfound energy came a confusing and weird spirituality. This involved, as far as I could tell, a mixture of referring to Dad as still with us and watching *The X-Files*. After an episode in which the ghost of a little girl keeps appearing to her mother, and the ghost-girl helps solve her own murder, my mother declared, "I believe that." I told her to hang a shingle, do some readings.

One night, my eyes shot open, awoken by what I thought to be, please God, a scantily clad and thieving nymph. Out in the yard, under the gently falling flakes, in her pale blue nightgown, my mother stared intently at the pink toilet, part of which had peeked out from the snow. The silver handle glowed in the spotlight of the full moon. I stood next to my mom in my boxers and slippers, glancing at her, then the toilet, then her. Her eyes were bright and fixed on the thing. She smiled a calm and all-knowing little smile, and a tear rolled down her moon-white cheek. I put my shivering hand on her warm and steady shoulder.

"Sweetie?" she whispered. "Did you hear it flush too?"

Simon moved into his new pad in the Fens that February. His bathroom had a claw-foot tub and a red hopper.
"Close but no TP roll," he said, indicating the thing. He
developed and framed all his toilet art, and they were the
first things to go up. Beautiful black and white and vivid
color both. Some shots of leaves swirling about the thing
went in the kitchen. Some of the thing half encased in snow
went in the hall. One with me reading the paper went in
the bathroom. He hung with care. The one picture of the
toilet in a lightning storm went in his bedroom. Last, he
placed an ancient photograph of us, the smiling family,
on his nightstand.

"So, that's how important we are," I said, looking from
the tiny ancient guy to the gallery of pink toilets.

"Nothing matters more. Come here." Simon must have
misheard, since he was spreading his arms for a hug.

———

God, my girlfriend sucked. Of course, she was on student
government. Of course, she was an A student at a ridicu-
lously competitive private school. Of course, she was pretty
and happy. Of course, she sang in the a cappella group.
Of course, somehow, she knew how to avoid looking like
an idiot while dancing. Of course, she was involved in the
theater department while balancing her commitments
to softball and field hockey. Of course, she founded the
all-female anglers society. Of course, she was a freshman
mentor. And of course, she sucked.

When she marched around the corner into Gleason
hall, where I was enjoying a doughnut, during one of my
free periods, I just knew that she wanted me to do something. And not anything useful, like make out in the music
rooms, but be productive or whatever, participate.

She smiled her hey-I-seem-to-have-too-many-teeth smile and waved an I'm-so-excited-to-see-that-you're-not-busy wave, which, frankly, I didn't agree with—the doughnut. She sat down and flung off her gargantuan purple backpack.

"Baby," she said, and it didn't sound sweet, it was a serious, business-baby. "There's a freshman boy whose father . . ." She trailed off, sliding her eyes around like fishing lures. "His father passed on."

"Bought the farm. Checked out. Kicked the bucket. Ate his last doughnut." I shouted them out while she cast treble hooks through me. "It's *died*, baby." I employed the business-baby, too.

"Fine. His father died. Anyway, I told Mr. Sweat that you'd talk with him if he needed to talk, and apparently, the boy wants to talk. Can you talk?" She grabbed my free hand.

"Mr. Sweat's first name. Is it Richard?"

"What?"

It took her a second, but when she got it, I was almost in love again. Soon enough though, she was mad at me like always: telling me that she was no longer asking, that I don't do anything anyhow, that I'm always hanging around after school, that I'm avoiding activities and home, that I haven't been to any club meetings in months, that the boy's name isn't Dick either, and that I had to meet him after classes, in the bio wing. Then, she was gone, off to her million other obligations, me being one that she was sucking at.

"This doughnut tastes bitter. And where's that side of betrayal I ordered?" No one else was free that period to hear my quips.

So, I found myself in the bio wing, surrounded by standing plastic skeletons, deconstructable mock-ups of human hearts and human brains, and big maps of the human body with red and blue veins squeezing pink striated muscle tissue. I was studying the urethra and bladder when I heard the kid.

"You Wesley?" the kid said.

"You the kid whose father passed on?"

He didn't respond. He just stood there, in the doorway, looking down and kicking at the checkered black and white linoleum with his bucks.

"You got a mom?" I asked.

He nodded.

"Brothers? Sisters?"

"Older brother."

"Man, do we have a lot in common. I got a mom, an older brother, and, of course, the dead dad. I got it all!"

The kid went and sat down at a big black table with Bunsen burners all over it. I sat behind the teacher's desk, spun a metal replica of an atom, then folded my hands.

"How's it been?" I wanted to hear that it was nothing at all; that this kid would just throw his sadness on his back and carry it off to wherever you take sadness.

"I hate everybody and everything."

No dice. "How'd it go down?"

"Cancer."

"Lungs? Muscle? Ear?"

"Brain." He fiddled with a Bunsen burner.

"Brain. Heart." I held up a piece of hippocampus and a left ventricle. "Both major players in the body. Both hugely important to human survival." I juggled the bits of organ along with a rubber large intestine. "Slow death. Surprise death. Still dead. We all bought a ticket, kid: a one-way ticket to the bone yard."

The kid just sat there, in his required school tie, looking down, looking scared. He was coming to me. Boy, was he lost, this kid, who was about to torch himself on the Bunsen burner because he was now a zombie. Just going through the motions. And why shouldn't he be sad? Why shouldn't he be scared? He obviously has no idea how to deal with having his life all flipped around and slammed in the toilet. Then flushed. Then plunged. He didn't expect that. He didn't deserve that. Just a kid, who got robbed.

Then, something miraculous happened. Someone, something, some god spoke through me. "Everyone finds some way to deal with a loss. My brother, for example, he has busied himself with a job, a goal, and has been doing his best to laugh at memories of his father. My mother, after losing her husband, she has sought some medical help, developed a connection to a power greater than herself, and she is essentially making it now. And they've done this on their own, found these solaces. Truth is, kid, this is kind of an individual thing, this coping with loss. There's no right way. And no one can help you find your way. Everyone has his or her own technique, method, or process. You can try to do what others do. You can observe what your mother does, but maybe it's not your way. Perhaps, for you, it will not come quickly, but listen: it will come. Try to believe: it will come." When I escaped my trance, it was just me and the fake human parts left in the room. I put my hand on a skeleton's shoulder. He wobbled.

That spring, when snow melted off branches, revealing oaks and maples; when icicles slipped from gutters and basketball nets; when grass rippled out in soccer fields and birds sang again, so, too, did the pink toilet bloom, emerging from its icy hibernation.

Everything would burn bright green that summer: the leaves, the blades of grass, the ponds deep in the woods. Simon would take a stroll in the common with a new girlfriend, who worked as a biomedical engineer, and he would be fascinated by the fact that she wore a lab coat and worked on curing diseases. Mom would renew her RN credits, start part-time at Mass General. She would make a meal that had frogs' legs. They would both come with me to Accepted Candidates Day at college and marvel at all the buildings and opportunities. My girlfriend would win several awards at graduation, wear special neon tassels, and lie to me, saying that she was most proud of our relationship. I would break up with her as soon as I got to school in the fall. I would meet girls that didn't ask anything of me, but just wanted to get drunk and get it on. I would bump a lot of speed. I would steal a golf cart from campus security, park it on the stage of the auditorium, and I wouldn't be caught for this. I would get by, majoring in business, and I would move close to my mother and brother after getting my BS. We would watch the Red Sox with new girlfriends. Mom would bring us good food to our apartments. She would meet another doctor, and he would treat her well and never make me or Simon feel weird. Simon would have a baby before I did, and he would name him after our dad. I would be his godfather and make jokes about the mafia. There would be new houses purchased. There would be new graduations to attend. There would be laughs, and there would be cries. There would be a world, and it would spin lazily through a black void.

And the pink toilet would grow pipes, roots into the soil of our front yard. Tall grass would grow up around it. Mom would place nosegays of daisies and yellow roses in its basin, a good planter. The pink toilet would be there every time I returned to my childhood home. My wife would joke that she needed to pee so bad that she'd use the pink one. Our Christmas photos would be taken around the pink throne. Thanksgiving cigars would be smoked around it. Somehow, the pink toilet would look beautiful and good in our front yard, after years and years and years. Most of the time though, we'd be too busy or far away to think about the pink toilet. And it would wait, through wind and rain and snow and lightning for us to remember. Everyone and everything would live long and happy and healthy. The toilet would live forever and ever in our yard. In our hearts.

Pink throne.

Porcelain God.

Stupid. Fucking. Thing.

GRACIE

In my insomnia, I waited for the digital 2:59 a.m. on my globally-or-atomically-or-somethingly-precise cell phone to change to 3:00 a.m. My wristwatch was behind, and I thought to synchronize all clocks in my place. But I heard this moaning out in the streets and looked up. When I glanced back down, the cell phone clock had flipped over. I bent my ear to the window.

It was this two-syllable moan. Over and over. Maybe not human, but something wrecked. "Gray-Sea . . . Gray-Sea . . ." I pictured a dog floating in the ocean, then a guy looking for the dog at exactly 3:02 a.m. in Inman Square.

I knew I wasn't sleeping anyway. I knew setting my clocks wasn't going to stimulate me much longer. And this guy, calling out, Gracie, again and again, was something to do. I pictured the guy. A lonely guy looking for his lost thing. I could help out. I wanted to know that this messed-up guy got her back. I needed to know that he wasn't going to crawl into bed alone tonight.

I tugged a winter hat on, grabbed my smokes, and pulled on my ripped jeans over my sweatpants. Then, I was out on the streets, stopping whenever I heard the guy's call, triangulating him. I reached B-Side Bar, but now he was calling from the basketball courts on Elm. When I got to the courts, he was moaning for Gracie at the little square at five corners. At the little square, he was calling from back at my place.

I lit a cigarette and sat on a bench, thinking that Gracie's probably having the same problem as me. How does he expect to get his dog back if he's constantly moving? Each time she goes to him, he's gone. Hug a tree, dude. Stay in one place. When I heard him call out again, he'd moved impossibly far from his last spot. He got behind me somehow, calling from blocks away, down by the Somerville line. I heard him again, and he was back in front of me, somewhere up Hampshire Street. Crazy. It was the same voice. What are the odds of two guys missing a dog with the same name? Then I caught my-idiot-self and realized it was two guys looking for the same dog. But the same voice called from the south, then again from the north. Four guys? I heard it back near my place again.

I pictured the guy on a bike or scooter or motorcycle or something, crying out for his lost love. This Gracie, this dog had become all the guy's losses—his dead mother, his job, the missed opportunity with some crush who left town, all his boyhood dreams. This Gracie was now the white-hot core of stuff. She better be worth it, I thought, and headed off to help find her.

I passed a couple on my way down to Harvard. They stumbled, tangling their arms in painful-looking webs, but they were laughing. I heard it again, "Gray-Sea!" The couple kissed each other sloppily and backed their way into an apartment building, where they would climb the staircase, a four-legged smooching machine, crash into their small but clean studio, and ignore the puppy and his slobbered tennis ball. Then, I wondered how Gracie got out. What was the problem, girl? He didn't leave the door open. No, he loves you. All he really wants is your happiness. He found you as a puppy, needing someone to care for, needing to absorb himself in someone else's wellbeing after a loss, to not get confused in his own thoughts. He was careful with you, thinking you were his one, believing it was good. You were sensitive—he knew this and loved this about you. How did you get out, girl? "Gray-Sea," echoed through the blocks again.

I gave up and lit a cigarette on the curb. My wristwatch read 3:34, my cell phone, 3:35. I was changing a name in my contacts list to Gracie, and about to hit Call, when a dog came running up to me. I shoved the phone in my pocket, chucked the cigarette, and spread my arms. "Hey, girl," I said in a traditional dog-greeting voice. She trotted, happy enough. We embraced. She didn't have a tag, but what were the odds? I sat down and put my arm around her, making sure she wouldn't be going anywhere this time. For the guy, I figured I'd stay put and hug a parking meter.

As with most advice I give anyone but myself, my plan worked, and the guy's voice grew louder and closer. He was going to find us. I was going to watch this reunion. I was going to tell the guy to get her a damn tag, keep her on a leash, fence her in, don't let her out of your sight. She's the one, and you've got to watch her all the time. But when the voice came from around the corner, Gracie struggled out of my grasp and headed off in the opposite direction. "Hey, Gracie," I whispered. She stuck her tail between her legs and looked back. "What the fuck? What the fuck's wrong with you, girl?" I had a quick thought that the guy beat her or something, but she was fine. She was perfectly fine. The guy obviously fed her enough and all that. "Gracie? What the fuck?" Then, in a snap, she bounded off, disappearing into the black forest of buildings beyond a streetlamp. She wasn't lost. She was escaping. Do what's right for you.

"Hey!" A voice shook me back to the present. I spun around and finally laid eyes on the poor sap.

I didn't respond. Who was I? I was just some guy, out in the middle of the street at nearly four in the morning. I could have been a bad guy, for all he knew. But he didn't seem to know much beyond some sad panic.

"You seen a dog tonight?"

"Dog?"

"Yeah, a white dog about this high?"

"I haven't seen a dog, guy."

He put his hands on his knees and breathed loudly.

"How'd she get out?" I asked.

"I have no idea. I locked up the apartment. She got into bed, and when I came out of the bathroom it was like she never existed."

"Maybe she's in your house still."

"I thought of that. Everything." He raised his face to the streetlight and closed his eyes.

"You'll find her. I'll keep my eyes out."

"Thanks."

I reached for my smokes as he jogged after her, vanishing at the same point she had. Before I had the cigarette in my lips, I heard him call from an impossible distance.

I headed back home. It had to be past four. I finally felt tired enough for sleep. I didn't want to go in, though, when I reached my stoop. I knew what wasn't in there. The guy called out again, from the north, then, right away, from the south, then the east. It's easier to find things in the light of day, but easier to search at night. I made my way west, tired and hopeful. I joined all the other guys in town, calling out, "Gray-Sea," as if it were a matter of finding her.

An Exact Thing

Since my fiancée and I seemed to be the last couple in the world to read the novel, we were sure that all the hype would have ruined it. There was not a chance that the hyperbolic reviews—in the magazines and papers, on the sites and blogs, from our older trusted friends and our even more experienced friends who had children, the married couples bent toward iconoclasm—would be perpetuated by us, we Johnnies-and-Janies-come-lately. No way our expectations could be met. We considered waiting until the novel was released in mass market paperback, until there would arrive a string of days in which we hadn't heard mention of the book, and when that happened, we would purchase *An Exact Thing* from a used bookstore, peruse it on a chaise with a cocktail, where a reader's expectations are reduced to mere entertainment, and the story must compete with the pool and sky and buzz. But Kathy and I were being excluded from conversations. Friends would speak the novel's title or recite a character's line, then another friend would shout: "Stop! Stop! Mitchell and Kathy haven't read it!" The reciter would then whisper the line's remainder, turn away from us, and declare, "Well, they must read it," before leading the conversation into another room and finally sealing the door between us, the reads and the read-nots. When we heard that around their twentieth anniversary, Steven and Lydia had not invited us to a party to discuss the book, we'd had enough.

The book's publisher had nowhere near the marketing budget of at least fifty other titles on the new releases shelf, but *An Exact Thing* remained the #1 Bestseller for the entire summer. It was a "small" novel, authored by someone who had written two even smaller books without commercial success but suggestive of great potential—a collection of stories, a chapbook of poems. No one knew these works. Out of print. They couldn't be found.

When we asked for *An Exact Thing* at the used bookstore, the cashier laughed. Apparently no one was relinquishing their prized copy. When we brought the books up to the register at the chain bookstore, the clerk asked, because he had to ask everyone now, "How many gifts does this make?" We hesitated. We were embarrassed to admit that this was for us, that we were new. But before we could answer, he warned us: "No one can figure out who Ms. Taylor was going to write to" and handed us our receipt. This hint, this reference, made little sense to us. But we remembered the reviews, which mentioned the execution of a scene that described "in achingly beautiful detail a hand reaching slowly, feebly, terribly toward a pen listing in an inkwell, blood leaking from a pointer finger." That must be the question of the story, we decided. That must be Ms. Taylor's hand in the scene. This must be the central choice of the story: Whom does she love? We were excited at a chance to solve this mystery.

Great novels ask questions. Great works of art understand the difference between vague and subtle, puzzlement and mystery, not knowing and the unknown. In this way, *An Exact Thing* proved, unquestionably, to be sublime. What was so fascinating, though, was the simplicity of

the story, how straightforward, how strikingly unstrik-
ing the moves were. It told the story. It knew it had one
to tell and went right after it. Wonderful exchanges and
lines, to be sure, details, moments along the way: Buck,
a poor and gentle old alcoholic character pausing after
pulling a can of beer free from the plastic yoke of a six
pack to recall twisting apples free from branches with
his deceased lover; Ms. Taylor mistaking, quickly, sunlight lying on a wide green maple leaf for brilliant snow
in July, revealing her split desire for both the younger
and the older gentleman; Clarence, the other man, don-
ning a black suit for another day of trading, folding his
unseen love letter into a pocket square. But to whom she
would write the letter and what it would say, finally, was
the entire story. However chilling and serious, *An Exact
Thing* wasn't without humor. The tale approximated true.
One scene was a meta-criticism of pat romance novels.
A character asked, "What author, living or dead, would
you like to have to dinner?" Another character answered,
"Danielle Steel: dead."

We got it. Not the answer to the final question of the
book. We understood why everyone had told us to read
it, why everyone wanted to talk about it. How readers'
interpretations could reveal so much of their true character. We had ideas of our own. After finishing *An Exact
Thing* for the first time, we read through the acknowledgments, through the author bio, read the blurbs again,
the reviews, read the opening chapter repeatedly, read
the copyright page, the legal disclaimers, the note on the
font. We looked up from the book in cafés and caught eyes
with other couples holding *An Exact Thing* in their hands.
They laughed, shook their heads, and dived down into the
words again. Kathy whispered to me, not lifting her eyes

from the page: "She's writing to Gregory, the valet. She loves him." I laughed politely, not able to place the likely minor love interest she was referencing. Ms. Taylor had a choice to make. A big one that she made only when it was too late. And we would never know. But we could believe whatever we wanted.

When we entered Steven and Lydia's apartment for drinks, before heading out for dinner, all of our friends, all these beautiful couples, greeted us with applause. We bowed. Lydia declared, "Welcome to the club!" We were accepted. We felt older. We felt the same age.

All the gossip about work—how LeReux was now likely having an affair with the receptionist; how the boss's presumed mistress inexplicably outperformed almost everyone who'd been at the office for twenty years and immediately took over as VP; how Steven joked about staying late one night to sneak into my office and go through my computer to see if I had been on sex chat sites instead of working—and all the gossip about home—how we were twelve weeks pregnant; how Steven's ex-girlfriend showed up one night, drunk, and proposed to him in front of Lydia; how their daughter was now in an open relationship with two men and one woman—this was all prelude, was all forestalling, was all bullshit. We wanted to know about the book. We wanted to know what we all thought. So, we finally began talking.

It was the kind of conversation you always wanted to have with your friends. A real discussion. There was something, *An Exact Thing*, that we were all passionate about, a piece of artwork, something that gave us real questions, a zeitgeist that we had all experienced. We felt intelligent, like people with something to say. Although Kathy and

I were the youngest and the only engaged couple, we believed we were now of value. It was possible—if we could
all work together, with all of our experience informing our
theses and all of our hearts in the right place—to come to
a collective decision, a truth, a universal understanding
of which characters belonged together. We could figure
it out, once and for all. Steven halted our feverish questions and claims by positing: "First we must decide why
she keeps the necklace Isaac made for her." We pondered
it. Fingers tapped the tabletop. Tongues prodded cheeks.
Brows wrinkled. No one laughed. No one guessed. And
then my Kathy said: "Who is Isaac?"

It is not a joy of mine to apologize for my fiancée.
She is not someone who needs a regular apologist. I am
just as young and naive. I could not remember Isaac in
the story either, but I was more reluctant than my bride-
to-be to announce my ineptitude for close reading, a skill
Steven clearly possessed. But when she asked a question
with such an obvious answer to readers of our friends'
caliber, I cleared my throat and dropped my napkin to
the table. Although her actions should not reflect on me,
it is my instinct to think of Kathy and me as one person.
It is as if the sounds from her mouth could just as well
have emanated from mine, given the glances I received in
that moment. I accept the fact that she and I are linked,
which is actually something I love. I did see it as an insult
to her that Steven chewed his well-done filet, and raised
an eyebrow at me, not Kathy. So, in defense of her, with
frustration for the dynamic, I clarified for her, to them:
"We don't know who Isaac *is*, as in we don't know his in-
tentions." This settled the table, or at least my stomach,
for the moment.

"Shall we change the subject?" Lydia suggested.

And we did, without anyone talking.

Great novels need to be read several times. The second time I read *An Exact Thing* was in private. I showered, dressed, ate breakfast, and kissed Kathy goodbye for the day. I took my briefcase, walked around the block once and entered a café kitty-corner to our building's entrance. I watched for Kathy to exit a half hour later, headed to her office. Back inside the apartment, I drew the shades, loosened my tie, and extracted *An Exact Thing* from the shelf. I entered the words in my stolen way. Great novels hide greater meanings in little moments. We may read a scene as simply character-building or plot-developing, a line as filler or superfluous. But great books measure every breath of a narrator, and the reader, being only human, does not realize the economy and layering in each phrase. The reveal in each word and each unmade bed. I knew I would read it several more times. I would find time, make time, hide away. The second read showed me so much that I had missed before. It was as if I had been allowed the experience of someone else's read. What is the best analogy? The book first shows its surface. The big idea. The second time, you follow a secondary character and see another story develop. You notice that a specific expression is used repeatedly, which you couldn't possibly catalog, reading it only the once. It's like meeting a person at a party. Then seeing her on the street. Then kissing her in the dark. Then lying to her. It's you, though. You are the changing thing.

An Exact Thing finally left the bestseller lists in the winter. Galley copies, early printings containing typos, European versions with varied covers, translations with newly intoned lines, review copies with missing page numbers, these sprouted up for sale by Christmas. Kathy and I exchanged coveted United States First Editions. We retreated to separate rooms, rereading before New Year's. The book remained novel, and I was delighted to find that in the first edition, my least favorite character, Jaden, an aspiring actress who seduced Buck and was the ruin of his life, was no longer a part of the story, and that Buck was not an old alcoholic but now a gifted nineteen-year-old cellist, studying in Vienna and falling for a prostitute.

Steven and Lydia had a party at the turn of the decade. Kathy and I spotted three iterations of the novel's dust jacket: one lying next to the television, one on the kitchen counter, and one half concealed under sheets in the guest bed. We asked, because we had to ask now, how many times had they read it? We admitted to repeat offenses, and to reading it in private, occasionally in secret, embarrassed to be discovered with *An Exact Thing* yet again by our spouse. No number of reads would have shocked. What was shocking was that Steven and Lydia had also kept their numerous reads secret. We crept back into the discussion again, the debate that had made us all so uneasy, back in the fall. Who belongs together?

Kathy, hardened by months of feeling foolish for her analysis of the work, her inability to read subtext and subtlety, hesitated but soon offered penetrating questions. I, now open to more and more interpretations, offered that I wasn't sure anymore if Ms. Taylor was the one about to pen the letter in the end. As far as I knew, *now*, Ms. Taylor wasn't even the protagonist. Her scenes had diminished over time, and in my last read I encountered her in only one sequence, as the flirtatious secretary of Mr. Janz, whose storyline had finally appeared to me in my third read and now seemed much more central than Buck, whose character had vanished in my eighth read. It was Florence in the end, the woman left at the altar. She had someone else's blood on her. It wasn't her at all, probably. It seemed possible to me. It seemed almost obvious at this point.

Lydia asked: "Who is Florence?"

As the coincidence of bewilderment registered with the group, I, now holier-than-no-one, shot Steven a raised eyebrow, not Lydia. I searched for his embarrassment. But he wasn't looking at me. He was staring up to the posts and beams, agape. He shouted: "How many times do we have to do this?"

I wasn't sure if Steven was angry with me for bringing up the book, if he was bored with the subject, or if he was furious with his wife for her carelessness. I apologized, but Lydia waved me off.

"We've had this fight a million times," she said and patted my shoulder. "You couldn't have known."

"I'm sorry. What fight? About the book?"

Steven growled and threw his champagne flute into the fireplace. He brushed by me, crunching the glass shards on his march to the kitchen for, presumably, something stronger.

Lydia stumbled into the dark bedroom. Then Steven emerged from the bedroom with a dustpan and set to sweeping up the mess. Lydia fluttered into existence in the kitchen entry, clutching a tumbler of amber liquor and shaking her head.

Kathy and I went home that night and looked at each other, wide-eyed, shocked that the debate over the meaning of a book could crack open a chasm between two intelligent, reasonable people, a couple that had been together for years, whom we looked up to. Great novels should create fans, theses, courses, and literary heirs, not separation. Great novels inspired the passion of those first conversations, parties, amusing and enlightening debates. Great novels did not divide people. I didn't know how *An Exact Thing* could possibly transform from a beautiful, tantalizing, endlessly intriguing topic to a source of pain and jealousy, to a blade. Kathy and I were on the same page.

So, I asked Kathy—after not having done so since defending her ridiculous question that first night—what she thought of the book. Now that she had been with *An Exact Thing* for so long, what were her feelings? Who belonged together? We were picking up blankets and folding them, washing dishes, turning on and off the faucet, putting glasses in the cupboard, unbuttoning and buttoning.

"I'm afraid," she told me.

I laughed. "You don't need to be afraid with me," I assured her, because we could tell each other anything, because Steven and Lydia were foolish for taking something made for entertainment so seriously, were foolish for allowing a stranger's work to invade their relationship. If something should enter our relationship from outside, if it was this story, however seductive, it should not ultimately matter. We made this relationship together. A story could not be more powerful than this bond. I would understand.

"Do you believe yourself?" my Kathy asked. "Do you?"

With hope that we both felt the same for *An Exact Thing,* but an irresistible and dangerous curiosity to discover that we did not, I said, "I do."

Test

Please get comfortable. Sit at your kitchen table, or in your favorite recliner with a surface on which to write. Once you've begun this test, do not get up, change seats, or take a break for any reason, unless the test asks. So, please, use the bathroom now, grab a glass of water, stretch, because this is going to take a while. When you are finished with this test, please place the answer sheet (and any other papers used for longer written answers) in the enclosed return envelope and mail it back to me. Do not use a pencil. No erasing. You must be absolutely alone throughout the test. If your phone should ring, do not answer. In fact, power down your phone now. If your doorbell should buzz, just forget about it. If it's important, they'll come back, or they'll leave a note if they are the note-leaving type. If you do not know the answer to a question, just try your best. Do not leave answer spaces blank. Turn all clocks face to wall or unplug them. And don't forget the clocks that may appear on your microwave, coffee maker, radio, or wrist. Lastly, try to enjoy yourself.

SECTION I

1. *Come here often?*
   No. Well, yes. I come here all the time, but I live here. This is my apartment. I come *back* here quite often,

to be accurate. Sometimes, though, I am here without coming here. It's just that I never left. So, like, yes and no?

2. *What are you wearing?*
My painting jeans and a red and black flannel. Of course, I'm wearing boxers, too, but . . .

3. *What do you do? Funny to ask that, but that's what we say now—not who are you, or what are your interests, or how do you like to spend your time, or what are you good at, but what do you do?—like your occupation is who you are. At least, at first.*
I am a house painter. But that's my day job. Really, I am an artist. Actually, I've just gotten used to saying that. *Artist.* But that is my passion—it is what I "do," but during the week, the nine-to-five, I'm painting houses, not canvases.

4. *Interesting. Do you find that line of work satisfying?*
Which one? House painting pays the bills. It's not "satisfying," but everyone's got to work. Finishing a canvas, though: that's satisfying. When I have an idea and then I complete it, when I've reached a stopping point . . . that's when I can breathe, have a beer, and feel good. You know, I never feel alone when I'm working on a piece. I am having a dialogue with someone. And that someone is me. The best conversation I could have!

5. *Are you seeing anyone?*
Not at the moment. I just moved to town about two months ago, left behind a great love. But I am an artist. I asked myself what was really important in life and came up with the answer: right now, my art is

important. People, I can take or leave. But I need to hone my skills, really do some great experimenting, great painting at this point. So, no. Sorry. Probably more than you were looking for.

6. *What is the difference between a duck?*

Seems like there's more to that one. A typo? If not, I've heard: the higher the fewer. That's a weird one! Maybe that's a perfect question. It screws with your perception. What is a question? You make me ask, "and what?" The difference between this "and what," "and what," and what?

7. *Just a question I like to ask. I feel there are some questions, besides name?, age?, hobby?, that tell more about someone. Like "Would you rather have a hand made of chocolate that would regenerate, or the ability to breathe underwater?"*

You're asking, essentially, would I like to be a pariah for the rest of my days, or have the ability to see worlds that no one else could see, the ability to enlighten myself, to see places that would make me cry, make me think, broaden me more than anyone could be broadened? I'll take the breathing underwater. And if you could supply some waterproof canvas and paint—look out!

8. *I don't like chocolate that much, but it's just the food I think some people would enjoy. I would breathe underwater. Imagine the dates you could have! If you and I could both breathe underwater . . . The kisses we could have! Sorry. Sorry. That was rushed. Do you like music?*

Who doesn't? I have tickets to see a show this weekend. I have two, but I can't find anyone to go with. Still out there, you know?

9.   *Me, too.*
     What?

10. *So, tell me about your last girlfriend.*
     That's a little awkward. Like you're not supposed to talk
     about politics, religion, ex's, right? Her name is Anna.
     Or should I say was Anna. She's not around anymore.
     Trust me. I am glad to be out of that one. As I said ear-
     lier: got to concentrate on my passion now. Sins of the
     flesh can wait. But I am a red-blooded, American man.
     I need my action. Sorry. That was tasteless, something
     I would have erased if I could erase the things I think,
     say, do, write, here. She does marketing for a tech com-
     pany. She's dedicated to her work, but I know she must
     have aspirations beyond that work that she doesn't find
     time to pursue. I can't respect that. A totally content
     person, who doesn't see that she's a cog in the wheel of
     crap, you know? And I couldn't stick around and let
     her dreamless life infect my hopes, make me think of
     my dreams as silly or something. We met in high school
     but didn't start dating until we were both out of col-
     lege. Best friends for years and years. I remember our
     first kiss . . . But I don't want to do that . . . remember
     all that with . . . you, you know? The bottom line is that
     it's over. Some people make a choice to live a normal
     life. A life filled with normal love. Others choose to be
     an artist. It's a sacrifice, but I know I have to make it.

11. *Come on. I'll tell you . . .*
     Wait. What?

12. *My ex was the only person I ever dated—high school sweethearts, al-
     though we saw different people at times. I never slept with anyone else.*

We have been over now for two years, and I haven't found anyone I really liked since. Since . . . well.

Jeez. Only one boyfriend, eh? That's serious. So, we have something in common. Lost love. Well, lost love sounds so dramatic. But that's nice to hear. That I'm not the only one.

13. *This has been fun so far. Why don't we get back together after a five-minute break?*

Oh, sure. Yeah, I need to do . . . something anyways. See you later.

SECTION II

14. *So, what have you been up to?*

I gessoed a canvas. I have been doing a lot of fantasy pictures, abstract things, but now I want to start still lifes again, possibly portraits. I could paint your perfect straight lines. Evoke the stark contrasts of black on white. Your 8 1/2" x 11" figure.

15. *Are you still wearing that?*

Yeah. So? You want me to change?

16. *Forget about it. Remember all that stuff you told me about your ex? Do you still think of her?*

No. I've already gone over this. I'm done with that. I'm here now. With my work, with this new life. With this test, this *you*. I'm not looking for anything. I had my love and all that. Now, I am onto something important.

17. *You're sure?*

I'm not doing this again. I refuse to go over this again with you.

18. *What is the true identity of a mirror?*
There's my girl! You know, that's an awesome question. Only you would ask that. You make me think, and think about my own work. You can never look at a mirror without seeing what it is reflecting, right? Then, I guess you can never see what a mirror truly looks like. If you built an airplane out of mirrors, would it be invisible in the sky, only reflecting the blue sky around it? They say that the artist's intention has little to do with the meaning of the piece. So, can you ever see the true identity of a piece of art? Of an artist? Of me? Good question.

19. *One or two?*
Two. Now. Usually it's one. But today it's two for me.

20. *My sister's still dating this asshole. He hit her again. I keep telling her to get out of there, but she says she loves him. What should I do?*
She has to get out of there. At any cost. Call the police on him, the next time you hear about this. That's awful. Inexcusable.

21. *You're a good man. I'm happy with you. Do you like me?*
It's nice to have something to do for once. All my friends are back home. I have to stop calling it "home." This is my home now. I came out here to see if I could do it without anyone else. I mean, an artist has to have his solitude, has to be alone. I want to see if I succeed. Without Anna, I am working more, concentrating on my dreams. But, I have to admit, I get a little lonely. But that's the pain that the artist must interrogate.

The other night, I wrote her a letter. I tore it up in the morning. A moment of weakness. She told me that she wouldn't try to contact me. She would give me space. Time, whatever. I am happy now. About you. Yes. I like you. I like the company. I like the challenge. But I'm not looking for anything. I have to be up front with you.

22. *Will you take me into your bedroom?*
 . . . Okay. I'm going to grab a drink first.

SECTION III

23. *Have you heard that you sleep with whatever you hang over your bed, that you are figuratively getting into bed with the pictures on your wall above your bed?*
 Yeah, I think I've heard that. Psychobabble bullshit. I'm my own man.

24. *Who is that?*
 The painting? That's from before I left. It's Anna.

25. *You must really be attached to it.*
 It's just a good painting, I think. A good likeness.

26. *What would you say if I said, I love you?*
 I'm glad I got a drink. "That's a roundabout way to say something like that" is the first thing I would say/ did just say. But then, I would be flattered. I am having fun with this. I wouldn't say it back right now, if that's what you're getting at. But do I need to say it, yet? If I do, if I admit that I've gotten attached, that I've found something out here, then it's just going to get messy. I just left someone.

27. *Can I stay here tonight?*
Do you mean on the couch or in . . .

SECTION IV

28. *What do you like to do for breakfast?*
It's all learned behavior. What I would like to do is fry two sunny-side up eggs. Toast shooting out of the toaster, landing on my plate. Jams in a rainbow burst of colors. I want orange juice squirting out of the faucet, coffee mug warm on my hands, steam rising, making swirls of cream, painting letters in the air: LOVELY MORNING. Bacon crackling on the stove, sending fat and grease fireworks over the rooster-shaped kitchen timer. Champagne corks darting around the room, off the fridge, where I have a note tacked with a Monet magnet that reads: TO DO: Smile, smile, smile. But, lately I have been sucking down cigarettes and drinking instant coffee while staring at my piece of shit paintings.

29. *Do you think you know me? You've never asked me anything about myself.*
I know that I like you. I know that it feels good to have someone interested in me. I know that I haven't felt like this in some time. I know that you have breathed some sort of life back into me—a life I didn't know I was missing. I know that before you started asking me things, I wasn't really thinking. I know that you make me like myself. And I haven't had a bad thought about you.

30. *Do you know that I have dreams? Do you know that I want more than just a good time? Do you know that I have feelings, too? Do you know that this isn't a one-way street? Do you know that I want someone to have an*

interest in me beyond me helping them? Do you know how many times I have started these things, and I become someone's mother, helper, whore? Do you know that maybe I need life breathed into me? Do you know that I'm messy inside and that I am not always a funny, quirky questionnaire? That I can be mean? Do you know me at all?

I am still here, waiting. I am still here with you. Isn't that enough? Why must I express a great interest, a great love? I am here, and, if I didn't care, I would have put you and this pen away by now. You know that I came here to escape just this type of situation. I can't get attached. I need to do my work. Why do we have to label things all the time? Can't we just have fun? I can't get that serious. I can't. I have a goal. And that goal doesn't involve another messy relationship.

31. *Why did you pick me up? Back then, when I first asked you about yourself? Why did you keep leading me on?*

Here's an example: Rasputin. He used to pick up prostitutes and sleep next them, to see if he could deny his bodily urges. He tried to do something, dare himself to try something that all his being was going against. I always do that. I tell myself what exactly I'm going to do. Like here. I am here to do work. To not get hung up and I am testing myself. I do like you. I do. But I'm just going to fuck up, either with my work or with you. It's all happening again. I'm failing.

32. *I know. I know. I'm sorry. I overreacted. Do you want to place a coffee mug on me, leave a dark ring at my edge?*

No. Of course not. It's just getting to me. I haven't painted in so long now. I've been spending so much time with you. I'm getting stressed that I'm falling for you. If that's true, then I have to break this off. But, no, baby. I don't want to make a ring of coffee on your edges. Here, let me rub out the folds in your back.

SECTION V

33. *I lied to you. Do you know that?*
What? You?

34. *Right now, I'm lying. I have been seeing other people. I am in the hands of 34,000 men. I am in the hands of women, too. And the truth is I love the attention. The only way I can be good to you is to be with other people. You make me so mad, because I love you and you don't have love to give. I want you, but in order to come back to you and not feel like an insignificant floozy, I need to cheat on you every second of the day. It makes me feel guilty, which makes me want to be tender to you even when you're being such a self-obsessed asshole. It's crazy, I know, but it works. I feel so bad about it that I have to be good to you. It was an experiment, a test to see if I could find a way to be better to you. Can we work through this?*
Well, this comes as a bit of a surprise. I mean, here I am, leaving behind my love for my art. Then, you come along and demand all my time. I give it to you, but can't give you the love you need. So, what do I get, just for being honest? I get someone who's off getting drooled on and fondled by the entire township. I just wanted something to do, someone to be with for a little, not anything big. I'm sorry what I wanted isn't exactly what you wanted. I just can't believe you'd hurt me like this. Lie to me. Discard me. Just split like this. I can't believe you'd go off and do whatever it is you do. Go off and screw other people, too.

35. *Do you deserve that?*

HOW YOU WISH

Birthday Cake Candles

Your first significant encounter with the rules of wishing came with the birthday cake and its requisite lit candles, the number of which denotes age plus a single extra luck or wish candle. This is typical. The scenery of the wish-situation has been fairly standard from your initiation onward through the years. Yellow teardrop flames atop stocky candles of primary colors, or atop stalky candles of primary colors. The low rumbling chorus of traditional song containing your name. The little warmth on the tip of your nose and your cheeks. Dark red faces closing in all around. Red-orange closed eyelids.

A rudimentary and erroneous rundown of proper wish behavior accompanied your earliest cake-candle wishes. The rules are—you might remember—Close Eyes, Formulate Wish, Open Eyes, Extinguish Candles with Solitary Lungful, Do Not Tell Anyone the Wish.

But what a bizarre (not to mention incorrect) set of rules! Didn't you always want to share the wish? But you were informed that if you told, the wish could not come true. Hooey! Nonsense! While you sat at the kitchen table of your childhood home, surrounded by all the loving persons of your young life, the burden of secrecy begot a confusing sadness of having to make a wish alone. Shouldn't the friends and family have wanted to share in and support your wish, especially on your day of days? This erroneous mandate of secrecy fostered a perverse and sad strain of wishes in your early wishing-life. The proper rules state: In order for your wish to come true, you *must* share it with another person, ideally a best friend (family members can count as best friends). The *sharing-with-one* rule of the cake candle wish ensures that—should it come true—the wish will not be something you would feel ashamed to indulge in once made public. Otherwise, you could get pretty weird with your solitary and secret cake-candle wishes.

So many of your candle wishes were made before you had met Melanie, before you had really met anyone *in this way*. Were those wishes wasted—and, if so, for how many years? You don't remember the wishes you made when you were, what— three, four years of age? Though you do know that you followed those early rules, with eyes closed, picturing little selfish dreams becoming little selfish realities. What did you want? Sports victories. Vanquished bullies. You were a kid. You didn't know Melanie then, nothing of this kind of floating of the heart.

Fortunately, tradition persists forever through the years. Today, as an adult, you have the chance to wish on your birthday—a chance that doesn't come every year, because in order for the wish-scenario to conjure and establish its powers, the cake and its candles must be prepared for and presented to you in secret.

Tonight, you are staring down a 25-candle lumen. Still a young man, but no kid anymore. It's time to get serious, time to take things seriously, you think. Tonight, this wish will not be a throwaway. Here, in your small but clean studio apartment in the city, the first place that really is yours and yours alone, you will not rush through the wish-formulation to satisfy the cake-presenters, your mom and dad, your sister, and friends as they demand of you, "Make a wish! Make a wish!" No. This time you take it slow. Thoughtful. This time the wish is for this girl, Melanie. You want her. More than that. You want something with her. You met Melanie only a week ago, but already it feels different. You didn't play it cool, not with her, because this wasn't a hookup situation. This wasn't an arranged date, no friends trying to set you up. This was random chance, a fate thing, maybe. She has lodged in new places in your chest and your head. You sat down next to a pretty girl at your local haunt, just a Monday evening after work. You didn't expect anything but a beer and to read more of your book. She was reading, too, and you couldn't make out the title. You hadn't seen her before. A vexing tattoo on her right forearm caught your eye. Nothing figurative. You wanted to ask what it was, what it meant, because you were curious, not looking for an excuse to chat her up. But if you did ask that, you'd appear to be asking for an excuse to chat her up. Damn society, ruining everything for you. Then your natural-self leapt out through all the self-consciousness, through all the society-consciousness, surprising you, as if you were being controlled by another dimension's wish for you to chat her up: "I was just sitting here, wondering what that tattoo was, but I played through all the reasons I shouldn't ask, and now I just want to ask what it is. What is your tattoo, if you don't mind?" She *smiled*! And then—*poof*—it was hours later, and you were still talking and smoking cigarettes and walking through town, and a voice in your head said, *Oh, this is my person*, and you were surprised by that but also immediately distracted by her again. You parted ways, and you got to the end of the block before spinning around and catching yourself and yelling, "I didn't get your number." Jesus. Think of it. How precarious these things are. You could have rounded that corner. *Poof.*

Since it is your own birthday, the wish must pertain directly to you. The birthday cake candle wish is not a time for selflessness. Altruism is lost on the birthday cake candles. In fact, the wish should be downright selfish. You are allowed this selfishness. Go ahead. It's perfectly proper.

You notice your wish feels real this time, because it could come true, because you sense an unknowable force in the world that you have somehow tapped into. Whatever it is, it feels like it is favoring you and Melanie. Tonight, you are wishing for this one to be the real thing. But you know it is. It's got to be. Stare down the candles' flames. Blow out the arranged fire.

The demigods of wish-granting get to work. But they are strict and they are vigilant. They are known to watch us for the slightest slip-up, the momentary carelessness with the rules, with the rituals. No matter how desperate your situation may become, you are no exception to the rules. Though, at times, they may seem to be, the demigods are not kind. Though, ultimately, you may curse them, they are not cruel.

Wishing Well or Fountain

Countryside wishing wells and their city-dwelling sisters—wishing fountains—are communal. Most of life's wish-situations are solitary. Although public, the birthday cake candle wish is made by a single person, not by many at a fixed location. This affects the wish rules.

The fountain wish may be selfish or selfless, but it must feel whimsical. While the birthday cake candle wish is mandatory and—so—often unimaginative, considering the wisher's limited time allotment for wish formation and stage fright at performing in front of flame-lit faces in a dark and makeshift theater, and while the shooting star wish is inspirational and inspired (rules forthcoming), the wishing well/wishing fountain wish is a bit hokey. It's a folksy thing, regardless of rural or urban backdrop. "Oh, a wishing fountain!" you might hear lilting from a nearby and delighted child. It's a cute thing. There is no obligation to wish when stumbling upon these wells/fountains, but there is a chance that you might miss out on an actually-functioning, water-based, wish-granting device. So, the pull to wish is always strong. It's important to take a contemplative moment and admire the sparkling pennies, nickels, dimes, quarters, and foreign coins sprinkled across the tiny sky-blue tiles that line the bottom of the fountain. Listen for and indulge in the calming plunge of water rushing into more water. Since these wishes must commingle (for eternity, you imagine, though only until the annual scrubbing by the municipal janitorial services) they must have common tone, must play in the same key. *Whimsy.* Imagine the bubbling dissonance in the fountain when a dime, carrying the wish, *Please . . . let the surgeon's hand be true when cutting out Robert's brain tumor,* is covered by a quarter, carrying the wish, *Please . . . let the Bruins take home the cup, baby!* Any demigod overseeing that particular collection of wishes is likely to shake its head in frustrated confusion and grant nothing. Keep the wishes in the communal fountain whimsical. Maintain tonal harmony among the chorus of coins.

Your relationship—your actual three-year romance—can, at times, make you feel whimsical. Melanie has morphed you into the kind of fellow who holds doors for and smiles at strangers on the morning commute. You can admit it. This relationship has transformed you into the guy who takes strolls on lunch breaks to watch the wind chase the high-up maple leaves, or regard the architecture of your fine city's stone churches and glass towers, or pause for public art, the sculptures in marble and metal, the graffiti murals in purple and yellow. You can find and love Love in so many of its forms now. You have softened to the idea of whimsy. Your cynical and single days would never have allowed a toss of a wish-coin, unless it was to wish away the stupidity of wishing fountains, how naive all those wishers seemed back then, when you had it all figured out, but really *before* you had it all figured out. Now, here you are, on the way to the grocery store, right smack in the middle of a relationship that has made you a true believer, thinking about how you have plans to get red wine and tacos at seven tonight and then head back to watch a flick at your new apartment you have with *Mel*—just drinks, dinner, and a glowing laptop screen in the dark of your bedroom. *Ahh.* The sweet realization that majesty lies curled up on the couch, hidden in plain sight among life's simple stuff! This new understanding that the oldie's radio station love songs are not, in fact, sugary nonsense from a lost, irretrievable, innocent era.

You know what's so true about this relationship? It's that you have fallen into the person you are, not the person you should be or the person someone wants you to be. Mel and you, you actually nudge your real selves into existence, encourage these forms out of shadowy recesses. The world is a brutal place, and up until meeting Mel, you did what you could to grab scraps of confidence, of usefulness: defense mechanisms that got you safely if sadly through social interactions and career obligations; worldviews borrowed from books and magazine articles that competed with something at your core but that you espoused with fake conviction. But now, *now!* You are becoming yourself. And you *get* it. When you are with Mel, you are not simply with another person; you are with a complex, mysterious, and evolving life force known as a human being. As she changes, and as you change, you are in love with the spirit, the core, some immutable essence that exists for eternity while masking itself in slightly different human shapes and looks year after year, as you both age and grow. Jesus, listen to you!

With a chuckle, you lose the last morsel of your old cynicism. This is the whimsy required. It's a great trade, you notice, cynicism for romanticism. Toss a coin. Wish for Melanie to say, *Yes.*

Coin value does not affect chance.

Shooting Star

The shooting star wish is perhaps the purest of all wishes. The blowing out of candles atop cake would be bizarre except for its long tradition; the expense of tossing metal money into small pools for fountain-wishing has been coopted by less and less magical fountains across the cities of our country (arbitrarily selected watery tubs, really). But when a meteor streaks across the black sky, burning white hot at a million degrees, come a trillion light years through the multiverse, wish-making feels innate, involuntary. The moment is all-consuming, the cosmic spectacle colliding with the sudden acknowledgment of your own tininess in space and history since the Big Bang. The sight of the shooting star conjures a wish, without any real need of thinking one up. Romantic wishes are most appropriate, though no wish is truly off-limits with the shooting star. Wishes for financial gain or anything similarly impure is frowned upon.

It seems important. It feels like something meaningful. You are by yourself. Here on a beach, in late summer, having escaped on this hasty retreat to a Cape resort town in its early offseason because you needed to fetch perspective on your marriage. You couldn't concentrate at work. Really, you couldn't face your coworkers who know Melanie. You lied and said you were taking an impromptu romantic vacation when requesting the days off, giving only a day's notice, to just get the hell away for a minute. Jesus. Nothing functions as it should—even your voice, it feels faked, your mannerisms, they aren't your own all of a sudden, playacted—when things are fucked up with Mel. The word divorce was used. It was actually stated as a real possibility, in the middle of the series of terrible fights last week. *Divorce.* If it happens, at least there are no children. God, what a freezing comfort. You used to brag about Melanie, about how perfectly fit you two were. How you both lucked out! You were once proud, without vanity, of how this relationship had navigated real problems with maturity, respect, and essential love. Friends and coworkers once sought you out for advice, about how it was that you and Mel had built such a good thing. How embarrassing to feel adrift while the folks who once needed your counsel now appear so much wiser.

You are facing a conflict too hurtful for even the two of you, however evolved, to smooth out and move past. *They didn't have sex.* You keep hearing yourself say this. You replay her words: *I caught myself. We didn't.* It is meaningful. She stopped it before that. The whole brief thing is a symptom. You've both ignored some shit. You hadn't been having sex, at least regularly. At first, of course, sex was all the time, then once or twice a week, then it was spread out more and more, but you were both really concentrating on your jobs, and your schedules weren't lining up, and she'd come home and you'd be asleep in front of the TV, or you would get up early and then make plans with a friend at night. You were traveling more for work, sometimes not calling before going to sleep in your hotel rooms. Sometimes, you were staying up at the hotel bar with someone and wondering. But you never. You both encouraged each other's careers and social lives that maintained your sense of individual self; you two weren't going to wind up codependent. That was a good thing. But for too long you left out the hard work of maintaining the romance, and now this. The cheating is a real shock, but it's human. You want to get through this. You do not want to run. Mel, too. She wants to work.

So, here you are on a beach, alone at midnight. Tide rushing in. Moon rising up. Cold sand in between your toes. Socks and shoes in hand, swaying, a bit drunk. Behind you, on the road, the sounds of care-free revelers roaring past in the last rented convertible of the season.

Then. A shooting star.

When you have been circling your thoughts and forgotten that there is anything in the world larger than your worst problem, that white streak across the sky feels like a ping from a friendly demigod who just happens to be awake and seeing you.

A wish for the strength to work through the impossible parts of love.

11:11

You must randomly find a digital clock reading: 11:11, and never await the flip from 11:10. The accuracy of the timepiece does not influence the wish. Of course, *time* is of the essence with this wish-scenario, having, at most, 59 seconds to formulate and express. The appropriate wish should relate to the particular day in which the wish is being made. Nothing long-term, nothing expansive and grand. Something concrete that could happen within the day. Of course, the ante meridiem 11:11 leaves more hours for things to happen. In the post meridiem, the wish can apply to the following day, though this diminishes chance. The 11:11 wish should be refined and reduced to its essence and whispered to yourself: "Nail the Presentation" or "My Son's Baseball Championship" or "No Cavities This Time."

It feels desperate and pathetic, but critical, to wish on 11:11 now. With Melanie sick like this. But you take any opportunity to wish. In fact, you have invented new moments to wish upon—2:05, her birthday, February fifth; 6:14, your anniversary; 1:13, your daughter's birthday. You are wishing all the time now. But at eleven past eleven, you hope this precise time of day holds more value, that it conjures and establishes powers, that it means more to the demigod in charge of the temporal wishes. Mel is sick. She has battled. She has done everything they told her. You have supported her. Your kids have been stronger and more helpful than you thought teens could be with sadness and emergency. You need to know the effort and attention worked. That Mel will come out the other side. She has gone in for the latest follow-up tests. *Please . . . let the results be negative, let it relent.* A wish at 1:13 a.m., at 2:05 a.m., at 6:14 a.m., at 11:11 a.m., 1:13 p.m., 2:05 p.m., 6:14 p.m., at 11:11. A wish on a ladybug. On a shooting star, though you find yourself scanning the night sky for them. Every wishing fountain, though not in any moods that could be mistaken for whimsical. A wish on every bird that flies overhead. A wish every time you see your reflection. A wish upon seeing the bottom of every pint glass, every coffee mug. A wish every time your kids hug their mother. A wish when the phone rings. Every time you pass through open doorways. Whenever a cloud moves in front of the sun. Each time she—. Everywhere— Anything— The same wish.

Wishbone

The practice of wishing on victorious wishbone battles should cease. If you find yourself pressured into the barbaric and passé ritual, instead of wishing, take a moment to consider the act of wishing in general. It is a regular part of your life. Wishes have marked your path. You have made wishes from the time you were a small child to today, a grandfather. Why have you wished? What's been on your mind lately, wishing these days for what? What have you wished for most frequently in your life? Is there a common theme? Think through the list—wishes for Melanie to like you, to love you, for it to be real; wishes for Melanie to marry you; wishes for the strength to work through the hard times; wishes for doctors to find cures; wishes for Melanie to feel no more pain; wishes for her, about her, on her behalf—you got so many of them. Did you deserve any of this? You feel that the demigods favored you, at least for a while. Or maybe it was that they favored Melanie, and you happened to benefit from being hers for so long. You can now thank them. And although the demigods turned their backs on you, you can now live with that. Yours would have been a shadow-life without her for all those years.

But do you really believe in some unknown force in the world? Isn't that foolish? Isn't it idiotic, in fact? The same sort of nonsense that idiots fill themselves with in order to ignore realities, hard truths about the way the world actually works. You are not religious. You are not spiritual. You do not dilute yourself. Sure, it's okay for your friends and your kids to believe in God, but you? It's irrational. But you have wished. You have wished throughout it all. Maybe it is time to disabuse yourself of that particular bit of nonsense, as well.

No wishing, this time. Think of your life of wishes, all behind you now, while you twirl a segment of an animal's skeleton, surrounded by grandchildren, there in your grown daughter's home on Thanksgiving, seated across the table from your grown son, the wishbone battle loser.

Eyelash

When staring down at an eyelash, the small black open parenthesis on the fingertip, formulate a magical wish. Remember, the eyelash is part of you. You send it off your fingertip and out into the world. The eyelash is the opportunity for impossible wishes, experiences and situations and ideas unachievable by the current laws of nature and

your own limitations. This is a time to be creative, imag-
inative, supernatural with your wishing. Think of flight,
of invisibility, of angels, of world peace, be altruistic,
think magically. Wish for signs and omens and divine in-
tervention. When thinking of the dearly departed, wish
for the peaceful rest of the parents and the grandparents
and the friends. When one is feeling less than useful to
the world, wish for the power to believe you are *enough*.
When society goes bad, and there seems to be no justice
or accountability, and people are mistreated, wish for a
changing wind, a new and beautiful world in its wake.
When feeling whimsical, wish for enchantments and benevolent sorcery to be real.

When thinking of Mel, wish for afterlives. Wish for
reunions in other dimensions. Wish for the spiritual and
the magic parts of our human imagination to have always
somehow known about what happens after. Wish to feel
her presence on a luminous pier. To touch her and hold her
again. To be held. Wish for a little more time together, on
that eyelash. It's perfectly acceptable to wish in this way.

You are alone in your living room, having rubbed your
eyes, in an attempt to shrug away a quick and sad flash of
memory. You see the eyelash on your fingertip, and the desire to make a wish floods your chest. It has been so long.
In this moment, in this living room, sitting on a couch
that Mel never curled up on, while you lift your head to
consider what you should wish for, set your gaze far out
through the bay window that she used to look through,
out beyond the maples of your backyard to some impossible distance. Steel yourself. Concentrate. Blow on the
eyelash. Watch it fly into the air and suddenly vanish into
life's history. Wish. Wish for wishes to be more than hope.

4.
EXPERIENCE SURREAL TIMES!

Out of Order

My life had turned upside down. I was at a loss; I had no idea what to do, what had gone wrong, had been going wrong, and, if I were to be honest with myself, I would have to admit that this wasn't new, this thing with Anna and me: this impasse—we were on two different planes. I was all over the place. My office showed the chaos—half-drunk coffees all around the computer, books opened to random pages, inkless pens everywhere. It was a mess, both my work and this thing with Anna and me. And I call it a thing because I wasn't sure anymore what exactly it was, what it had been, what it was becoming. Not too long before the day I'm describing here, I thought I would get down on one knee. I was at the age, with the same woman for years. But it was madness: she was mad! Telling me that she couldn't look me in the eye anymore. What was that? What had I done? I hadn't the foggiest. There was nothing that could be done that day. So I stormed out of the house, yelling back something about having to clear my head, get things together, and I made more promises about how I would return after I figured everything out. By the time I came back, I would be a saint or a psychologist, at least, and we would fix everything up right. Turn this thing around.

My initial instinct was to take a walk, just stare at leaves on the sidewalks, thrust my hands in my pockets, and, with luck, wind up at the edge of a Zen-pristine lake, where everything would become clear—where everything would be lined up properly. There, I would see how to fix it. In my haste, though, I had slammed the screen door and emerged into the chilly, early-November upstate New York day wearing only an Oxford shirt, no coat, no hat. To return indoors and fetch my sweater and gloves was out of the question. I couldn't give her the satisfaction of my mix-up, proving to her that I had made too much of a show with the exit and all. I decided to brave the chill. Maybe it would freeze and flake away some of the clutter in my brain. But when I slipped my already frostbitten fingers into my pants pockets, I discovered I had the keys to our car. A walk? A man needs to drive! Engine humming, downshifting, scenery racing by. Of course! I would drive fast, take lefts, rights at whim, and still end up at the lake of reflection and clarity. I ripped open the driver's door and eased into the seat. The engine roared to life. A drive. Clear my head. Figure it all out. Outrun the confusion.

A late lunch, a turkey club—it didn't sound grand and romantic, not as romantic as the idea of hitting the road, doing some soul-searching, soul-cleansing. But, still, hunger is hunger. After I eat, I thought, I could do all those great feats. People go to coffeehouses for all sorts of reasons—to work, to chat, to eat, to drink, to think, and, possibly, to clear their minds. When things go south, everyone offers each other tea. "Your fish went belly-up? Have some tea, dear." "You can't decide between this job or that? I'll put on some tea, we'll figure it out." "Your potential fiancée is, all of a sudden, mad, and your thoughts are all over the place with, what, work, your upside-down relationship, and you're out in the cold in a button-down? Tea. Tea for one should do."

A slight comfort came to me when I remembered a student who had mentioned that green tea was beneficial to your brain or energy or chi or some such nonsense that was important to your well-being, so I ordered a cup. A placebo for the mind. A good kick-start to fix up the old discombobulated brain.

The tea and sandwich came to $9.51. When I placed a ten-dollar bill, two quarters, and one penny on the counter, the tattooed barista hesitated, eyed me suspiciously. I smiled. I like using change—that's what it's for, that's its proper function. Get rid of the clutter and jingling in the pockets, clean out the baggage. Change only ends up on the floor in the car anyhow.

After the turkey club, which was delightful, by the by, I sipped the, by then, cooled green tea, which turned out to be Earl Grey. I didn't let it get to me though. I wouldn't let such a small thing bug me. There were bigger, badder matters all stuffed in my brain. A small mix-up. I said Green, she heard Grey. I convinced myself the sounds were nearly indistinguishable. An honest mix-up. Green. Earl. What's the difference?

Back on the road, headed to god knows where, I arrived at a fork. I put on my blinker and decided to venture left to where mountains loomed in the distance. But the lever got stuck down, and instead of starting the left blinker blinking, the radio began sputtering mindlessly. I jammed the lever back up, and the radio dial stopped. An unexpected mix-up, probably just some loose wiring. I assured myself it was nothing.

I did myself a lot of good by driving well over the speed limit. When you're doing 20 over the suggested rate on a country road as the sun is setting, there isn't a whole lot of

room to think about your ailing relationship with a mad-
woman, a woman who now seemed unpredictable and crazy.
I imagined all the papers in my office, all these fictional-
ized photos of Anna and me looking sad and messed up,
all my anxieties put down in documents, and all of them
clinging for dear life to my bumper, but giving in to the
gaining force, tearing away from my mind. I passed cars
over the double yellow. I blazed past cows that moved too
slow to see my speeding capsule whiz by. I liked the feeling and pushed the button to roll down the window. The
window switches, however, decided it would be better if
they now controlled the dome light. I fiddled with the
locks, which only brightened the indigo backlights of the
speedometer. I clicked the dome light on and off in rapid
succession, and, with this newfound order, the windows
finally shimmied downward. The car had gone mad! All
the wires were crossed. Okay. If everything was going to
entangle itself in a mad haywire bonanza, so be it. The
windows were down, the car was flying. I was feeling better. That was all that mattered.

A scenic view somewhere in the Adirondacks tempted me.
A green sign with white water ripples. My lake! I pulled
onto the gravel shoulder, removed the key as if from the
stone. This action sent the door locks into a flurry of
gunfire. I jumped. The buttons for the doors did not respond to my request that they, for the love of Pete, just
open up, and I escaped through the window. One other
car was parked on the shoulder—a brand-new red Jeep.
Through the driver's window, I spotted a blue flashing
light. An alarm system, no doubt. Everything working in
proper order there. Lucky bastards. I stared at my maniac
car, nodded to the Jeep, and suggested some note-taking.

It's no help to see people in enviable positions when you're trying to sort things out. I needed there to be no one else in the world at that moment, but there in front of me was a young couple cuddling by the railing, facing my lake. The young man in a warm-looking blue fleece getup stroked his companion's back with the regularity of a pendulum. A chill ran through my body as I placed my arms over the railing, giving a small wave and silent *Hi* to the couple when they looked me up and down. I faked a yawn—I don't know why, just to be doing something, maybe to suggest that I was just taking a breather, not, in fact, wishing them into oblivion so that I could think of what to do with my scattered, upside-down life. I dipped my head to peer at the blue-black lake, my eyeglasses promptly diving off my face and falling, falling, turning and turning as they plummeted and splashed into the lake below. The young couple followed my specs' descent, and then they looked at me with wide eyes. I smiled again, gave a tiny wave, and went whistling back to my lunatic car. "Hey, guy! Did you need those?" I heard the kid yell. Need my glasses? Noooo. No. What for?

Now, my vision blurred, my anger with myself growing for not finding a place to collect my thoughts, I clicked the remote keyless entry button and my car's windows thought to shut themselves, and the trunk, god love it, opened suggestively. My car was all in shadow at this point. I clicked and clicked the button, yanked on the door, but nothing was working. Nothing was wired properly, nothing was fine. Still, I hadn't figured out what to do with Anna, and I was terrified to drive home in the dark without my glasses. Defeated, I climbed into the trunk, pushed down the backseat, and noisily struggled through the narrow passageway to the cockpit. I stabbed the keys into the ignition, promised the vehicle I would change the oil on time from now on, and the trunk, with whatever logic, slowly dropped and clicked shut. So be it.

When the rain started, I pulled the wiper lever. A tape ejected from the deck with the force of a champagne cork, ricocheted off the rear window, and pelted me in the back of my head. I hit the scan button on the radio, which made my seat recline; I reset the odometer, which flicked on my hazard lights; until, finally, in the blur of rain and glassesless eyes, I honked the horn, and the wipers went into godsent arcs. But only five arcs per honk. I got looks from everyone who passed me; my hazards were on, I was driving well under the speed limit, squinting, and blaring the horn for the wipers. This was the way of it for the entire drive back into town: rain; cars honking back at me; me, mouthing, "It's my damn car!" until I switched to, "Count your blessings, ingrates!"

I pulled into a gas station and asked the attendant for advice on my inexplicably crossed wires. He looked down to the engine and battery and things. "Any trouble with the tumblers?" he asked.

What tumblers are, I cannot say, but I nodded that yes I did see problems, many problems with the tumblers. Well deduced, sir.

He reached down to the battery, yanked up a blue wire, reattached it to some hidden location, and wished me luck. I gassed up the beast, thinking that was all it needed. I imagined, as I sprayed gasoline into the tank, that the coolant was just as rapidly squirting into the oil pan, the oil pan dumping itself into the console's ashtray.

Before I could return home, before I could face Anna, I had to try to find some way to gather myself, collect my thoughts, figure it all out. I crawled into the car through the window, put the car in gear with the temperature controls, and headed for a bar. I had wasted too much time with the green-tea fiasco, the juvenile joyride, the scenic view, which had, with such wit, stolen my sight, and this haywire car.

I backed into a spot on Main Street and thrust open the driver's door, refusing to deal with the windows. The rain was still coming down, and my white Oxford was stained gray, sticking to my chest. I barged into the bar, wild-eyed, and ordered anything on tap. People go to bars when they need a drink. And to need a drink means to have something amiss. I had never done it before, but I had heard the idea. Bogart ordering whiskey and soda after getting slapped by some dame. The sage barkeep. It could work. A drink. A drug, really, to clear one's mind.

An elderly couple in a booth across the room clinked two wine glasses, and I gave them the evil eye. How do you get there? *There* being probably their 40th anniversary—still in love, still finding that when their faces changed, when things started to get different in life, when work demanded more of your time, when the idea of kids entered the picture, when actual living kids burst onto the scene, they could still find the beauty in the newly forming lines about each other's eyes—how do you do that? When in my early 30s, when Anna and I were about to call it quits, where would I be? Back at the beginning. Everything upside down. The barkeep pulled the tap for my beer, and I sprang out of my stool, possessed. I ran, doubled over, to the bathroom, and quickly relieved myself under a sign that read Out of Order. Where had the attack come from? I couldn't place the logic of anything anymore. Alone in the bathroom I regarded myself in the mirror. I was blurry. I couldn't make out the distinct features of my own face, but it was me. It was a little off, a little skewed. Soaked through. A little mad. It was me though—blurry and confused, unhappy and at a loss. I thought of the young couple at the lake. How did they do it? Were they meant for each other and so could enjoy themselves? The older, white-haired couple clinking glasses. How? I pushed the button for the dryer and imagined my crazy, maniac car roaring to life and leaving me here at this bar: the thing laying rubber in circles at some far-away track. All I wanted was some space to fix up my mind, and here I was, soaked through in a bar with nothing to return home to but the same mess I had left. Maybe worse now. I wanted to expel my helplessness. I placed my hands on the sink, bent over, and tried to will out a tiny cry. The toilet flushed. Inexplicable madness! I turned the faucet and tears flowed from my eyes. I wept into the basin. Nothing was working right.

I ignored the barkeep's yells as I ran out the door. I needed to get home and fix my life.

Now either I'd completely lost it, or my car actually had hightailed it off somewhere. It was dark, and maybe I just couldn't see it without my glasses in the rain and the wind blowing bags and leaves in lamppost-sized tornadoes. In any event, I started running down Main Street, arms in front of my face, turning sideways into the headwind, rain running off my chin in a solid line, my shirt pressed to my chest and the tails flying out behind me like a cape.

The strangest stuff. As I ran, squinting, I swear I made out a door two stories up on the face of a building. A pickup truck speeding in reverse through a red light. I saw a birch tree blown to the ground and daisies ripped up and rising into the moonless sky.

At the corner of our street, I caught sight of a rainbow fish swimming uphill in a flowing puddle. The wind and the incline forced me to a walk. I bent over and grabbed at the air, pulling myself up the street. I peered into the window of a house and, under the bright chandelier of the dining room, saw dunes, a sandstorm.

My car was in the driveway, dry as a bone under the carport. I made nothing of it. The screen door flew open, banged against the house, flew back, and was made a toy by the wind. I shivered and grabbed a hold of the knob, turning. Locked. I slapped my pockets. Nothing. I pounded the door, yelling for Anna. I rapped and screamed in the sideways rain.

Finally, she cracked the door and stood in her white robe, her pretty head hanging down, refusing to look at me. She seemed unaware of the storm. I called her name. She did not look up. She did not back away from the opening. I yelled to her, "Anna!" She was right in front of me. I banged on the house. In the wind and rain and madness I screamed out to her. "ANNA!" She remained staring down, unmoving. I was not welcome. But I did not go. No. Not right then.

I put my arms down to my sides. I hung my head. Then, it all came clear. I lifted my finger to the doorbell, pressed on the concave button gently, sensually, pushing inward, sliding my fingertip down its slick face with all my love. Quiet. Anna lifted her beautiful head, and her eyes, now on fire, blinded me.

Ready Set

You made it. Good. I need your help with this, friends. Mom, just stand back, don't worry. Okay. We're here in the field where I first kissed you, Laura. Remember? You see the cyclical symbolism to this spot? A first and a last. Here, in this endless stretch of toxic green grass in every direction, help me set the scene. And, just for depth, for one moment, take in the brown tepee, frosting-topped mountains lining the northern horizon, defining an end to this place. Hey, that's great: the two porcelain-white clouds have arrived. Notice how they're strapped like cottony earmuffs on either side of the sun, the sun that is tacked to the circus-tent-blue sky like a yellow button. The clouds look just how I wanted: one comedy face, one tragedy. You can see it, right? Just look, think, think of me, think of how you feel about me. I am leaving. I am taking off this very minute. It is good and bad. Good for me, maybe. That's what we think, say, repeat. Got to go. I have a destiny. Sad, though. Definitely sad. We know that. The truth is always a mixture.

———

Now, hand me that ladder, Jack. Perfect, an eighteen-rung wooden job. Set it here, right in the middle of the field. Oh, Laura, don't be sad. Here, quick hug. You'll see. This is going to work. I just want it to go right. Now, Adam, I am going to climb this ladder, and when I do, I want you to remember every time we died laughing—all at once. A good memory to recall is the time when you walked into our apartment, and there on the black and white checkered kitchen floor, I had laid out a full outfit of my clothes in a human shape: empty, armless, blue button-down shirt, one sleeve bent into a wave; empty, feetless black shoes pointed outward below the bottom of my empty, legless jeans; and an empty, headless hat and wristless wristwatch set to midnight, and I groaned from the living room, hidden from you, "I melted, dude." I melted away. Or when we were on the balcony, and you showed me some constellations, and I shouted, upset with wonder, "How could the Milky Way belt be our own galaxy!" Like, how the fuck can we see what we, our own planets, our own existences, our own little lives are inside of? And you explained, pretty nicely, that it is like sitting in the shallow end of a pool and looking straight out. You can see the whole pool: surface, bottom, sides, but you are also in it. You said, here we were, looking up at the deep end of the galaxy, straight out to the end of everything, staring up and out, far . . . staring at the end, the other side, the great beyond, from this little warped balcony, just us . . . drunk. You ended it with "drunk," and I thought that was perfect, because we were there, and we were doing all that big, cosmic shit, but we were also just drunk, you know? So, maybe, start with one of those two memories, where we laugh together. A tiny joke. A grand, godlike guffaw.

This goes for all of you: each and every one of you has a teary, perfect, sentimental, but also funny and really real letter hidden under your pillow. So just when you think you've heard the last from me, I'll slay you all again with a torrent of unabashed emotion, saying everything we couldn't in person. It is tactfully written of course. I'll be the last thing on your minds as you drift off to dreams of us getting together again to do something normal: get a beer, or just sneeze and notice that I am right there to say, "bless you." I'm right next to you in an everyday situation, buttoning my shirt, smiling. But this dream of normal hanging out will feel like our own secret hiding place, a secret ghostly feeling of home, of comfort. You're going to see me wink at you in your dreams for a long time to come. I hope our dreams mix. I hope I wander into yours, when you dream of me. I'll take over my part in your dream, because I'm dreaming of you in that same, lovely, normal life we had. A fantasy phone line crossing of dreams. Dream that I float in through your open bedroom window, that I smile at you . . . Remember me . . . ?

———

Mom, I need you to be filled with pride now. Proud, remember. You're thinking of me getting on the bus for the first time in kindergarten. You're saying goodbye to me, going off to do the ten hundred things I've done and that you've eased me into, with worry, but pride, remember. The ideal face for this moment is one that is starting to be overcome by tears of joy. This is my destiny. Picture me: here, look through the frame I'm making with my fingers. I'm draped in medals, on center stage, inside a stadium that is so grand that the dome touches clouds, and it is full up, all full up with fans, reverent students, professors, government officials, news teams, and they are all hushed, waiting for me to speak to them, but all I do is thank you, Mom. Thank you, Mom. You were the one who got me here. Without you, I couldn't have dreamed of all this . . . and all that. Your little boy is a man. And you've always got something on me, because when the milkman came, and I opened the door, and he handed me the bottle of milk when I was, like, three years old, I dropped it and it shattered on our foyer floor. I cried, feeling like I was wrong, and you comforted me, explaining that I was okay. You were a little taken aback by my reaction, but you taught me that lesson that so many people don't understand. Move on. No use crying. Unless the tears are triumphant, proud tears, like you are conjuring now. Good. Good dress, too, Mom. Simple, elegant, black. Your hair is catching the wind very nicely. Good. The age-lines on your face are all the years I owe you. I will get it all, and I will give it back to you. Know this. Perfect. Stay there, a little behind the crowd of my friends: Adam, Jack, and Laura. You can easily take a step back and let me go. Perfect. Hold it.

———

Your job is tough; I'm not going to lie, Jack. But if anyone can do it, it's you. Here, take this rope and grapnel. You are the strongest. You always were the best athlete. Big, blue varsity letters on your jacket. You're precise, too. Always teaching me a game to play, beating me, encouraging me to get better. Remember when we made up those, like, soldier-war courses in my basement, with tennis balls flying through the dusty light; old, crumbling desks and chairs acting as barricades over the concrete floor. We invented a point system for advancement and retreat, where the goal was to grab the flag and get to the end without the other shooting you down with gun-shaped hands? Remember? I do. You always won. I would slump over the dusty cardboard boxes, filled with dusty photo albums, falling slowly across long-neglected weight benches or sofa arms leaking their fluff. I wilted, collapsing, clutching my chest in the dusty light of the moldy basement. We've known each other for so long, man. Somehow, we stuck with each other. How? With all those other friends fading away and away, one after the other, we stayed together. How? Wonder about that as I climb the ladder. But then shake your head, say, without words, with only a gesture and moan, looking down, kicking a rock: "I guess this is it. All these years fly. Go on, good soldier." You, too, buddy. Then, at that moment, you must heave the rope and grapnel up over the sun and snag it good. It has to stick. It has to support me. The rope is long enough; I've measured it from the top of the ladder to the sky. This has to happen before the earth rotates, and the sun gets too close overhead. I need a good fulcrum, enough tension to yank me away. So, don't think you can overdo it. I know you can do this. You are an honest, workhorse friend. Anything for me, right? You are capable. I always envied your determination. A big compliment that I want to leave for you. Wherever I wind up, whatever I meet out there, know that I believe you could be doing what I'm doing, but doing it better, because I trust you more than I trust myself. It's okay to get cheesy. This is it, man. You big lug, you got a job to do. I'm stepping up now. When I am standing on the top rung—you know the part with the little warning against standing up there—that's when you must heave the rope, hook the grapnel into the sun. You see it, right? Look right at it. Let it burn your retina for a moment. Blaze this image of me into your head. I'll be silhouetted, but I will be smiling about our friendship. Do something big in my absence. Here I go. Handshake when we should've hugged.

———

Last night, we did it right, friends. I'll pause on the third rung to say this. Last night, the night before I leave, we just sat around with some beers on the kitchen floor, backs resting against emptied cabinets and emptied drawers, looking over photos with turned-up edges, laughing, and telling stories. No one mentioned what we all knew: I'm gone in a day. We just wanted one more night of goodness. And it was. I'll touch my heart now to show you all that I'm serious, that I'm touched. Another good night to take along with me. Adam doing that trick with his eyes, where it looks like they're gone, rolled back in his head. Jack extinguishing everybody's cigarettes when he notices they're not quite out, always helping to see things through to their proper ends, snuffing them. Laura informing us of how the French philosophize our climaxes—*les petites morts*. Good work, friends. And, Mom, a last good home-cooked meal, your chicken and mashed potatoes, a joke about me having to eat more vegetables, as if it were a concern now. Did you really think you could convince me, even now? Our good dog begging for table food. Me giving it to her, with a wink—I mean, what could you do? I'm leaving. I can cheat a little. Then, you sitting me down—serious for a moment—giving me a feather, mentioning how you have this thing about feathers you find, which I never knew, all this time, something that has to do with Dad. After he died, you started seeing feathers everywhere and collecting them. A piece of heaven. He's okay. We're okay, aren't we, Mom? Well, that feather is in my breast pocket, and if anyone asks about it, it's personal, it's family, it's a keepsake from my mom, and somehow, from Dad, too. Yeah, that's from Dad, too. Enough feathers make a wing. I'll believe in this with you. It is good to believe in something spiritual, I think, now. Thank you for everything. For the good and the bad we shared. You were there. I hope I was there for you. A son who knows his mom like a grateful cub, like a friend when the leaves fall and nights end with embers.

———

Okay. Laura, do you know what to do? Because I'm already up on the third rung. When I get to the fifth, you have only a second to touch my ankle before I'm out of reach entirely. I won't be looking for it, because by that time I will have resigned myself to leaving. Break your countenance, run forward, and touch me, turn me around for a kiss, one last one. For God's sake, there are never too many last kisses. I will wish that you would spin around, letting me see every side of you. Your face, your friendship, your intimacy, your hair, your newness each time for me. Let me see you in the ways I've seen only one person. Spin every which way that I know I love. One last time. So, remember, fifth rung. I won't be thinking of it. Maybe you'll whisper into my ear, with your hands clasped, resisting the urge to grab me down, "Stay . . ." But that's up to you. It would really add to the scene. If you do say it, I'll say something like, "Oh, baby. I'll come back for you." I won't know, neither will you, if that is true, but it could be. I'll hope and you'll hope, while I'm up on the fifth rung, that it will come true, but after that, we'll just have the guesses at night, the sappy songs that make us believe for another sharp shining second.

I'll miss you, though, baby. I love tracing your back with my fingers, our little game of spelling out words on your spine that only you can understand: "Soul," "Mate." How funny it is to remember how we met. At high school. I had fainted right there on the bench while we were waiting to go home after school. You gently woke me, introduced yourself. Funny how people meet and then how they end up in love. End up in the middle of a hundred loves with one person. Isn't it? Time flies. I'll remember your eyes, close to mine, while kissing. Yeah, I do open my eyes. Your closed eyelids pressed gently over a kissing, joyful face. I'd sink into the sand with you. But I've got to do something now. You're in here with me. Remember, fifth rung. XO, baby, XO.

———

Jack, you hold that rope taut when it comes to it. Laura, you know your part. Mom, stay there, just like that. Adam, when I'm at the top, I want you to wave. Just wave, because we're cool, man. We've always just been cool. Nothing fazes us, right? This one does, but we're going to be very cool with this one. We will smile, separately, someday, secretly, thinking that we were better friends than we ever let on. So just wave. Play it cool, bro. Here I go. But, just as I leave, you got to take that boom box, hit play, place it down on the grass, and let that beautiful song, the song with that triumphant climax, play so loud that the speakers rattle. I want that beat and those chords screaming through that little boom box we used to take to the park. So just hit play. I've cued it all up. A perfect soundtrack. Me, up there, a silhouette against the sun and sky, with those notes floating around us all. And just when the part comes that everyone closes their eyes to, the part where everyone bows their heads for a moment of silence, when everyone imagines the earth exploding with heart-shaped paper-cut-out fireworks, I'll be gone. You'll drop your head on the one, start to hum the notes, and on the two, you'll look up, trail off with the humming. I'll be a dot on the horizon. Be cool, man. Here goes nothing, right?

———

At the first beat of a song's beauty burst, the bass drum—BOOM—do I know my part? It's the easiest one. Tug the rope: it's sturdy, has weight, so thick and strong that my fingers don't touch my thumb. The rope, it stretches impossibly high, up and out. I can feel that the rope has impossible tension, a tremendous force, aching to yank me from my spot. All I have to do is hold on tight, pull myself up an inch, maybe less, get my heels up, get onto my toes, and place my feet in the air, and the rope, the anchor, the momentum, the power will do the rest. Then, all I have to do is close my eyes, breathe, feel the sharp, quick sinking and rising, the up and down of my stomach as the wind rushes past my face fast and loud, feel the creaking power of the enormous rope, hold on tight. Speed. Out and down. And then all I have to do is let go at the top of the pendulum's arc, let go and let the force fling me up over the mountains, arms stretched. Fly. Just let go. Just pull up. Just step out. Just say goodbye. That's all it takes. There's nothing to it, really. Everything's in place. Just go. Just go. Just let go. Step away: it will work. Say goodbye. Look over everyone's face. Look. Smile. Just let go. Blow a kiss. Go.

ORAL

He's down there doing his usual, which is a mix of entering her with his tongue and vaguely kissing her pussetta stone, and she's up there doing her yoozh: moaning with head back and eyes closed, really trying, but they both know where this is headed: nowheresville.

Wes gives up before losing all feeling in his jaw. "Did you?" he says while swiping at his cheeks with a fist, a moment he's always found awkward.

"I don't know what's wrong with me." She places her palms flat on her forehead, elbows to the slowly spinning ceiling fan.

Tonight's sex-kerplunk caps off only two weeks of anticlimax, but they've already established it's her fault. He's got a suspicion, though, that Anna's just protecting his feelings of inadequacy. He's gotten her off before, and, on the flip side, even her worst, seemingly obligatory trips down have eventually finished him off. It's mysterious.

"I want ice cream," she says, sitting up in sudden determination.

Wes hears: I want to scream, but quickly realizes sex is no longer on her front burner. "I'll get it," he says, buttoning his shirt. "Just wait. You stay."

Then, Wes is reaching for the keys and feeling Anna's eyes on him as he walks out the door.

Beholding the colorful array of ice cream brands and fla-
vors, Wes drifts.

If she really wants babies, it's not very persuasive to
suddenly go frigid like this. One day, they're twenty-
somethings having a roll in the hay, the next she's talking
about growing old together, teaching Junior how to throw
a curve. He wasn't expecting that.

Plus, there's nothing less sexy than babies. He's not
ready. And "babies" makes him think of his and Anna's
bodies as biological things, things that are for procreation.
He shudders at a lightning-quick *Miracle of Life* flashback.
High school Growth Education class. Placenta?

She mentioned the B-word in bed of all places, too.
Maybe it wouldn't bother him so much if, right after she
brought the whole thing up, he didn't thoughtlessly blurt
out, "I want kids, too." He's always erred on the side of
being a liar rather than admitting he's a jerk. But maybe
it isn't jerky to have a fear. Something will go wrong, if
he is a father. If only he had some patience, some nerve.
If only he thought about the ideas, expressed concerns. If
only he were honest with her. This lie, this crime of non-
passion, it's crawled into bed, gotten between them, in-
terrupted lust like a child.

At the register, Wes discovers he's got Rocky Road.

Apart from Anna's not getting off anymore, there are
other new features in Wes's world. For one, the new girl
at work has an ass like an onion, making him cry each
time she picks up an errant pencil off the newsroom floor.
His eyes have increasingly lingered on the escort classifieds that he lists for the *Weekly* and started seeing an en-
coded message in their breast sizes: "DD," "E," and, once,

impossibly, "DDD." Anna's emails now contain links to Most Popular Baby Name sites.

Joe, the copy editor, takes cigarette breaks every 30 minutes, and Wes starts bumming. One day, Joe waxes expert on oral.

"You spell out the alphabet," he says, pulling a Newport from his lips.

"Out loud?" Wes asks.

"No. No." Laughing. "You just trace the letters while you're going down on her."

"And that works?"

"Yeah, and it keeps up the variety."

"Genius."

"G-E-N-I-U-S." Joe speaks each letter while licking his knuckle. "I copyedit, bro: I know letters."

"What's with the menthols, Joe? You been institutionalized or something?"

"I'm a reliable source, dude."

"Word."

———

Wes runs through his ABCs ten times without so much as a yelp from Anna. Then, he wonders if it should be in lowercase. When Anna's still not screaming that certain scream that Wes needs to hear, that sweet release that he is beginning to forget the sound and feel of, he traces the letters in NOW-I-KNOW-MY-ABCs-WON'T-YOU-COME.

Anna lifts his head and looks at him.

"Nothing?" he asks, but he knows the answer.

"Come here." Anna pulls Wes up to her and places his face on her collarbone. He swipes at his exposed cheek. "I just can't focus on that right now. It'll pass."

Wes is thinking that Joe is an idiot. "Sorry, I was try-ing something new."

"Wesley, baby," she begins, and Wes knows that this is going to be something not about sex, but about love, and he's just going to wait it out, seeing as how it's all a cover-up for his stupid alphabet fiasco. "The most important thing to me is that you love me and that . . ." And Wes is right, and he stares at the door. What was it before? How was he able to do it? He reaches under his tongue, mas-saging the tender tether of muscle that holds his tongue back: it's tighter, sore. His tongue wants to retreat. He hits a tiny tear on the tether, and his tongue shoots back. "Be honest," Anna says. "Do you want what I want?"

"Of course, baby." He tastes blood; it hurts to form the words.

——

Anna's waving at a toddler at the coffee shop while Wes wonders why he's never been able to picture having a kid of his own. It's natural. People start asking if a baby's on the way. Wes's mom is too curious. Anna's older sister's got a bundle of joy for her mom to spoil.

"That is the cutest thing." Anna sips her chai tea and indicates the goofy little kid with the sippy cup. "When we have babies, I'm going to fill bottles with milk and tell them to wander around the house and bump into things for Mommy." Wes looks at the kid, and the kid cries.

"Fucking adorable."

"Wesley!"

"What?"

He shrugs and pulls out a pack of Newports.

"You're smoking again?"

He's not getting into it with her. He lights up.

There are self-fulfilling prophecies. His friend, Earl, always said that if he were to have a kid and the kid turned out to be *special*, he would give it up for adoption, arguing, "I'm not going to dedicate my life to something like that." Anna was there when Earl said this, so, of course, Wes told Earl that he was heartless and that all children are blessings. They were still courting. But then, Earl's kid *was* special.

Thing is, though, Wes really can't envision a child. Not anything about the idea. Is he sterile? All the pot smoking in high school, all the Mountain Dew consumption in college? He forces his creative mind to imagine himself in the hospital room, wearing the green scrubs, the nurse handing him his own swaddled infant. Wes watches himself tug on the soft blanket to see his newborn. But he can't reveal his child's entire face. In glimpses, he catches fangs. Yellow eyes. He hears a growl.

"What if I can't have children?" Wes asks.

"I doubt it, lover," she says and glides her foot up his calf. "But, we'd adopt."

"What? And get some monster!" Wes gets a slap on the shoulder, but he's serious. He can't picture being a father to his own son or daughter, let alone someone else's.

He's convinced himself it's not cheating: it's a test. He lied to Anna, saying that he had to meet up with Earl for cards. He actually said the word, "cards," which he's never met Earl for, but it worked. She believed him, or maybe honesty is going undetectable. He's at a club. A meat market.

Coming to places like this, to pick up, years ago, used to be a constant struggle with how to act. Wes had tried it all: buying drinks, pretending to throw around money; playing it cool, as if he didn't want to get any; lines; all of it, but he notices that entering a club, armed with only the thought of servicing a willing woman is working like fly tape. He regrets, for a second, not having this state of mind when he was screwing around.

"You're sexy," says a girl with gigantic yellow hoop earrings.

"You should see me dance," Wes agrees.

"I'm a cheerleader at BC," she proclaims, possibly her pickup line for older men with assumable fantasies.

"Let's see if you can keep up, then."

It's freeing. Wes does the robot, which he can't do, but Hoop Earrings loves it, because she's wasted.

Poof. They're at her apartment.

Smooch. They're on her couch.

Grope. Her shirt's off.

Finger. They're in her bed.

"Now, Shelly," Wes starts to explain his test.

"Rebecca."

"Whatever." He pushes her pom-poms onto the floor. "I am going to go down on you, then I'm going to leave. That's all this is."

She sits up, suddenly sober. "What is this? Are you a lesbian?"

"Yeah. No. What? Listen: Will you just let me do this for you? Will you tell me how I am? I want you to have an orgasm. Not that I think you would, but will you just not fake anything? Is this simple enough?"

Rebecca considers this long enough for Wes to start thinking she's a police officer. "Okay," she says, finally, falling back, laughing, suddenly smashed again.

The cheerleader's sexual routine is confusing to Wes,

with all the clapping and chanting for Eagles' touchdowns. Wes traces out the alphabet, at first, but then begins licking out words that run through his mind. True words. Real things. Brutal honesty. I-AM-CHEATING. I-WANT-NOTHING-TO-DO-WITH-YOU. YOU-ARE-NOTHING-TO-ME-SHELLY. SORRY-I-MEAN-REBECCA. YOU-ARE-A-TEST. And when he's finished spelling out how tired he is and how he's disappointed in himself for smoking again, he hears her yell: "GIVE ME AN O! O! O!"

So, it isn't all his fault.

Wes tells her to stay in school, then he splits.

One night, Anna's got her shirt off, holding her breasts, inspecting them. Wes watches this with mild curiosity over his laptop.

"They say that your boobs get bigger when you have a baby," Anna declares.

Anna's a C cup, which Wes likes. He's dealt with A's, and once a DD. Usually boobs are a pair, but he can only recall the larger set as two entirely glorious but separate entities. "I love your breasts, babe."

Anna puts on a T-shirt and says, "What are you reading?"

"The *Weekly*'s listings."

"Checking out your work?"

"It's so fucking weird: the whole world is in the classifieds. There's everything from 'Alex and Sarah Peterson married' to '$6 hubcaps for sale.' I look at the whole world every day until I'm typing someone's holy matrimony with the same enthusiasm as some scam run out of Seattle for telemarketers or mystery shoppers—I look at the stuff that makes life worth living right next to the bullshit that makes life inane and absurd. Real love and con artists."

"Wesley? Are you okay? You love the listings, I thought."

"I don't know. I just get confused sometimes about what matters, what's honest and good and what's just some more junk."

Wes catches himself and tosses the laptop onto the couch. He leans over and pulls Anna to him. He clicks off the light. They stay quiet for a time. In the dark, in their bed, in their apartment, in their little life, he traces words on her back, like they used to.

"See if you can tell what I'm spelling."

"I love this game." Anna yawns.

Wes feels tender for a moment and traces S-O-R-R-Y on her back.

"I love your hands. That feels nice."

"What did I spell?"

But Anna's asleep already.

"Do you know?" Wes stares at the door until he slips into dreams.

———

After staring at yet another day's emails of things to list: marriages, real estate for sale, medical studies, Fantasy Fulfillments, bartenders needed, apartment rentals, drummers needed, psychic readings, pot legalizing rallies, cuddle parties, I Saw You On The Subway love connections, used cars for sale, lectures at Harvard and MIT, and babies' births; after smoking menthols and seeing Joe, the copy editor, each time; after asking him if he actually does any work at the paper at all; after listening to the BC Eagles beat the BU Terriers 21–10; after thinking about Shelly or Rebecca or whoever sleeping with someone new; after talking to

Earl about how he's never had a poker night and maybe would like to have one; after telling his mom that there's no baby on the way; after, finally, clicking on the Most Popular Baby Names website and checking how far down the list the name Gun is; after reading the week's paper and seeing word after word after word and not knowing what anything means anymore; after tracing TONIGHT-IS-THE-NIGHT on the roof of his mouth so that only he could feel it; Wes heads to the adult shop.

It's arresting, the sheer onslaught of colors coated on the paraphernalia of sex. The fat brushstrokes Wes sees in the purple, red, and neon green dildos, vibrators, pocket pussies, on the packaging of lubricant, the sticks and blocks of incense. It's new and tempting, the caresses of feathers, tails of whips. And the names on the videos and magazines: GONZO, HARDCORE, KINK, and ORAL. There are red light bulbs for sale in this blue store. He sees rainbow arches of condoms. Wes sniffs the edible panties. Everything under the sun. Anything to get that certain scream from Anna.

He carries a mess of color and sex to the register, pays, and marches out, not at all self-conscious.

———

When Anna returns, Wes has transformed their apartment into a sex cave. He's on the bed, naked, under the glow of a rouge light bulb, in a haze of perfumed smoke, with the porn scenes flashing on the walls, surrounded by sex toys, waving her into the room.

Anna melts into bed, and Wes slips her clothes off, flinging her panties onto a blade of the slowly spinning ceiling fan. There's no talking. No words. Before anything

starts, Anna's already breathing heavily and flipping her
hair around on the bed.

Wes is made of pleasure from his loins out to the tip
of his tongue. He kisses Anna from her chin down to her
breasts, to the ridge of her hiphone. He gathers himself for
a moment and begins with his usual down there.

She's up there doing her yoozh: moaning, head back,
eyes closed. But it's still not happening. Wes will not
stop, though. He will not fail. He goes through the alphabet, for variety. He traces I-LOVE-YOU. Anna touches
his ears, tugging a little; she wants him to stop. She just
wants sex. But Wes spells out: N-O. She lets go and moans
again. Wes licks out the words. He lets go, too, finally, and
traces it all on her pussetta stone. The letters, the words,
the truth: I-DON'T-WANT-WHAT-YOU-WANT. Anna
thrashes. I'M-NOT-THE-MAN-FOR-YOU. Her breath
quickens. I-CHEATED. Anna grasps the sheets, twisting
the fabric into nipples. I'M-LEAVING-YOU-ANNA-I'M-
LEAVING-YOU. And Wes hears, at last, what he's needed—
that certain scream, that sweet release.

Kind Eyes

You could steal stuff if you had a car waiting. Late at night, the families were asleep. No one knew you were in there, would even dream it. Quiet town in summer, unlocked front doors, open windows, garage bays like yawns. I never took anything though. I was always more an observer type.

I slipped into this stranger's house through a side window. I was on the way to my mother's, back in town to see her. The layout of this stranger's place was like all the others. Every one of them was the same thing. A colonial, two rooms deep on the first floor, dining room to kitchen, living room to office, office to deck. I could feel everyone sleeping, up there on the second floor. It had been seven years since the summer I turned eighteen, since I was last here, going through strangers' homes, but that stillness, that calm of the place felt exactly the same. Photos and notes about phone calls covered the fridge. "Excellents" ran down the list on a report card, except for one "Satisfactory" in Spelling. Still, though, pretty good. The first-grader probably had the first bedroom on the left upstairs. One of the photos showed this family in front of a seawall, but all wearing jackets. Mom, Dad, pink-haired girl, beaming bowl-cut boy, who I could've been. They maybe asked some guy at the beach to take the photo. I get asked to do that a lot. Somebody once told me I have kind eyes, which I took to mean I look too naive to know how to steal, how to hurt someone. Maybe that's why I never felt guilty for looking in places I probably shouldn't.

A list of chores on a kid's chalkboard showed Jessica hadn't emptied the dishwasher. I pulled down the door, slid out the rack, and grabbed a white mug with a sketch of a blue whale. Before I opened it, I knew which cabinet the mug belonged to. Every place was the same. I took my time, moving the plates and glasses and silverware to their cupboards and drawers. They always said no one got broken into in my hometown. Me, I never broke in. Everywhere was wide open.

A game I used to play was to see how close to the sleeping kids I could get before getting too scared and booking it. To check if I could do better now, I climbed the carpeted stairs. On the landing, two doors faced me, but, just to see, I rounded the banister and made for the master bedroom instead. I pressed my ear to the door and heard snoring. A dead sleep. The mistake some people make when sneaking in or out is to open the door too slowly, trying to will the hinges into silence. But to kill the creaking, you have to throw the thing open in one quick sweep. I grabbed the doorknob and pushed into the room. The door brushed the carpet, making a sound like a sharp inhale.

Real late at night, houses never get fully dark. Even with drawn shades and a dull moon and low clouds, somehow a little light spread out, and my eyes adjusted. The mother and father faced each other in their sleep, not touching, but like fetal position and facing each other. Sometimes you could see a thigh, a breast. I could have done anything to them, unconscious below me, right then. I could've stolen the wallet off the dresser, flicked on the overhead light, freaked them out. It's something to realize what you can get away with, that you have the tools to hurt, to hit, to scream, if not the will or want to. But, like I said, I was a watcher. I just looked at them: a mother and father sound asleep together. Just to see, I reached out and stroked the mother's hair. She let out a two-note sigh.

Before closing the front door, I leaned in and shouted, "Hey! Lock up!" Then, I booked. I shot a glance back to see a light on upstairs. It would be denied down to a dream. Nightmare. No one would notice the blue whale mug and the emptied dishwasher. Even if one of them did, Jessica would take credit and begin an okay relationship with small lies.

———

It was after midnight, and my mother would be comatose no matter when I showed: witching hour, lunch, dawn— she was on her way out, I had heard—so I went to my old friend Pete's. He worked at the town's restaurant in winter, the golf course in summer. One of those guys with a lot of potential in high school and just like couldn't hack it after. A guy like that, you hope he didn't notice that the compliments stopped coming, or that at least a girl would someday smile by his side while he told a story. But Pete thought I was the crazy one, for taking off. I was "misguided" for going away.

I peeked in through the dark windows at Pete's. I knocked without even trying the knob. A light clicked on deep inside. Pete appeared in his doorway, a massive silhouette. Then, he was hugging me and slapping my shoulders.

Pete cracked two beers, and I told him about the house and family.

"Jesus Christ. Do you still do that shit? You shouldn't do that," he said.

"It's not how it looks. And, no, it's been years."

"Still, though. You're like a peeping Tom. Your eyes aren't for some things. You got issues, man. I always said you had issues." He was beaming at me, pointing at me.

I watched a car light sail across Pete's living room wall, up onto the ceiling. Slow. Then gone.

"You see your mother?"

"Not yet."

"See her. You'll be sorry if you don't."

"I'll see her," I said.

Visuals flare up, die down. Images demand you look, then you get fooled. You got to be ready to look, to be nice to whatever you see, but then you give up because there's too much. You check out a girl getting dressed with her hair up in a towel and think of comforting morning rituals. You watch a balloon float up and hope the kid's not too sad. You spot a romance book in a stranger's kitchen trashcan and hope they know actual love. But you got to ration. Some things can empty the well. You got to look away.

I got sick of looking at Pete, living his little life in his little place, and found a house with a glowing window. I knew the house, the family, on my street. They had older kids, but I guess they sold it because these were young boys, hanging out in the lit-up room. I started a cigarette, watching them do the same, pass it around, and bend their heads to the open window. Then the light cut out. I figured they heard footsteps in the hall, but a minute later they creaked the front door too slowly. One of them, maybe the one who lived there now, spotted me. They formed a tight wall, staring me down. I stepped onto the black-green grass.

"Hey, guys," I said, and I looked at all of them at once. When they didn't respond, I figured I was scaring the shit out of them: I would be the mystery man, the outsider, who snuck into this town and terrorized young boys. I pictured it on the news, on the firsts. So I added, "I used to live up the street. The Nelsons, you know?"

"Where?" said the one who I guessed lived there.

"Twenty-four. Cardinals on the mailbox." And, hearing this proof that I was local, they calmed down, or the weed was mellowing them. There was no bad man in this town, no thought of the possibility for long.

"You want to see something?" one wearing a backwards hat asked. And the group headed around the house, into the woods there. I followed a safe I'm-not-going-to-kill-you distance behind. They unearthed a cache of sparklers, firecrackers, bottle rockets, roman candles. Each grabbed a weapon of choice and continued through the trees until it opened out to a dark field. The sounds of the night-cars rolling on the highway now came to me, like ocean waves.

"Won't that wake your parents?" I asked, peering back through the trees.

"Maybe. They don't pay much attention," said two of them.

The first bottle rocket went up, cleared the treetops, and became an invisible whistle for a moment. Before the little rocket exploded, I scanned the stars, thinking nice thoughts about fate and meaning-making, that long ago some big thing decided I should stay away from this town. I thought about my family, how my father took off, too.

There weren't bad men around here. Then, after a joyous *POP*, my eyes swallowed the weak purple beauty-burst of childhood pranks that littered the black sky and erased the stars.

"It's the fear of getting caught, isn't it?" I said while they shot off roman candles. Roman candles don't make much noise, though. They sound like spits. I thought I heard police sirens, way off.

"Jake got caught last week," said backwards hat.

"Fuck off." Presumably, it was Jake who said this.

"Jerking off in the basement."

"Shut up."

"You'll all get caught," I said.

"Not me," said backwards hat. "I do it in the shower."

"Even there," I said. "You get seen. It won't matter though, if the person's like me."

"What's that mean?"

"I'm good. Decent. I know what to look at, maybe, or look for, so no one hides."

The boys weren't interested in me anymore, though. They burned the sparklers and whipped the white-hot embers at each other. Eventually, they were galloping off, away from me.

I headed back through the woods and saw lights go on, then off at Jake's. I thought about waiting a little while, sneaking in through the back slider and watching the rest of the sleepover, a childhood event I knew I had experienced but couldn't possibly remember, because my eyes would have been shut.

———

Someone had actually locked the door at my mother's house, so I slipped in through the porch window. A strange, professional-looking woman slept in the living room. Folded shirts lay next to her, along with needles and prescription bottles on the coffee table. I felt like I was in someone else's house again, the fear of her waking up, seeing me and calling the cops. Even the framed pictures, I didn't recognize them right away. I grabbed one. All of us, before Dad left, after I graduated grade school or something meaningless. Now it was Mom's turn to go. I told the Hospice lady I'd just be a minute, but she didn't stir.

Upstairs, I lay on my old bed, pulled back the curtain, and stared out to the neighbor's house through the trees there. I felt like I had snuck back after being in so many people's homes, after looking at trophies in dens, china in glass displays, souvenir magnets of zoos on fridges, calendars with tiny birthday cakes on birthday days, like when I was young. I had done it, got back in my bed without getting caught. I was here with my mom, after looking in the places I shouldn't. But I still wanted something more.

I threw open the door to the master bedroom with one sweep, which my mother did not hear, or she was too almost-gone to notice. She lay on her side of the bed with more than half the queen-size empty. A stuffed teddy bear with a scarf sat next to her. Did she hug that, in the night, and believe for a moment someone was with her? I stared down at the scene, took it all in. My mother was always pale, but now she looked so white she was see-through, made of light. She breathed thin scratches. I could have done anything right then.

I wanted to crawl in and make up a bad dream to tell her about. I wanted to feel comforted by her once more. It seemed foolish and pathetic, and she didn't need to think her son was unstable right before she sailed to the other side.

"Hey," I said. "Hey, you there?"

She just kept breathing, kept living a bit longer. I climbed into bed and lay on top of the sheets. I curled up. "Hey, Mom," I said, and I watched her eyes flail under her white eyelids. I saw her. Slowly, I reached out and touched her cheek. Then I jumped out and swiped the house key off the dresser in one quick silent scoop.

I went out the way I came in. On the porch, I took one last look. Then I stabbed the key in the door lock, opened up the place, and took off.

———

Sometimes, I like to remember that after I split, I spun around to see a light on upstairs, that I watched as my mother forgave me with some beautiful gesture, and that I nodded knowingly. But I don't think anyone would believe that. My mother finally went a few hours later. I spent the night far away. First in a neighbor's foyer. Then somebody's bedroom. Then a kitchen. One onto another. I flipped through piles of photos. I watched parents dream. I drew birthday cakes on calendars. It wasn't that good though. Before I left town, I saw Pete again and told him to find a sweet girl and to get too busy to remember missed opportunities. He just shook his head and laughed, but he hugged me. Taking off, on the bus, I watched out the back as my old town's green street signs grayed, the grass yellowed, the black tar went white, the blue colonials dripped sick green, the lid of a trashcan blew off and rolled to the edge of the world, the fading pink skies began to erase telephone poles and brick chimneys from their tops down, and the already-vanishing everything else back there dissolved away. But I always knew that would happen. Kind eyes get used up.

Used Goods

I needed a lot more than what I had managed to cram in the back of my Subaru for the move. It was a hasty job, which wasn't philosophically conceived—I simply hadn't thought the move through enough. But I recast my anxiety about leaving things behind into a dream of starting over. I took my clothes. Some books. A few lamps. My computer and guitar. But I left almost everything else on the curb with a sign reading: "It's All Yours Now!"

Right across the street from my new apartment, there was a used goods store. Perfect, I thought. What do I need? I made a quick list, and I promised myself I would only get what I wrote down. I was only going to get what I needed this time. No more clutter. Bed frame. Work desk. Chair. Kitchen table. Pots and pans. Bare essentials. A clean slate.

But you never know what you need until you are faced with all the things you want. Nearly everything on my list was in the first room of the store, so I told the nice people working there that I would be buying these things and coming back periodically to cart them away. Then, like a fool, I browsed.

I've always liked secondhand stores. Antiques warehouses. Thrift shops. The kinds of places where you might find a gleaming set of silverware in a mahogany box for hundreds of dollars on the same shelf as a tape deck missing the rewind button. You might find a bargain, or an item no longer being manufactured, or a toy that you had misplaced, years and years ago, a lifetime ago. The toy could be the very one you played with. It had its own lifespan, just like you. And here you two are, coinciding again. I always enjoyed that the items had other people's stories and lives imbued in them. Someone may have used the desk a century ago to write unrequited love letters by candlelight. I try not to get carried away, but I wonder and hope that something lives in the material.

I pushed through a beaded curtain into a second room that housed cardboard boxes of VHS and cassette tapes, VCRs and radios, standing lamps, nightstands—actually I needed a nightstand and forgot to jot it down—shelves upon shelves of old novels, glassware, cookware, paintings, armchairs, jewelry in glass display cases, magnifying glasses, large standing brass ashtrays, rotary phones, vinyl records, and dusty turntables. Some alluring nostalgia. Useful but mostly unnecessary.

The third room, which lay behind a heavy oak door, contained much the same as the first, but these particular items, on closer inspection, were damaged. A desk missing a drawer. An upright piano with only black keys. I suppose one could take this stuff home and fix it, but I am no good at repairing anything. Better to move on.

I creaked open a beat-up screen door to enter the final room, which looked just like an old general store. Aisles stacked with cereal boxes and soup cans. Refrigerators filled with liters of milk, bottles of juice, cans of soda, cartons of eggs. Frosted, brown bottles of beer in six-packs. I deserved it, I thought, and pulled open the glass door. Refreshing icy breath escaped the cooler. When I grabbed and lifted the six-pack, I tumbled backward. It was incredibly light. The bottles were empty. Caps sealed to the tops. I held a bottle up to the light. Empty. I replaced the pack and grabbed another. Light as the first. It felt good to hold the six-pack of empty bottles. It felt manageable. I felt a touch stronger, a bit more capable. I carried it around the store, thinking I would inform the cashier of the beer problem when I was finished shopping.

On the other side of the registers were long tables with board games laid out. A Scrabble board with words on it, a completed game—STRETCH, perpendicular to HIRE, perpendicular to EXIT. A notebook rested next to the game. Initials were scrawled on top, and scores were written down in columns: "J.M." had beaten out "W.M." and "R.P." by 20 points. Two tiles lay in the tiny wooden rack on one side of the board, and one tile lay in the rack facing me: "M" (three points subtracted from W.M.'s score). I put the notebook in my pocket and gingerly picked up the Scrabble board, balancing the game on my palm like a waiter.

At the impulse-buy section by the counter, I saw mason jars of Bic pens without caps. Blues. Blacks. One red. There were yellow Post-it pads covered with words: "TO DO: Laundry, Groceries, Oil Change." Some words were scratched out. I placed the six-pack on the counter and withdrew a blue pen. I tried crossing off "Laundry," because I had actually done it already. But the pen was inkless.

The old man in line in front of me paid for a pack of cigarettes, opened it, and tapped out a crumpled filter into his palm. I bought the six-pack, Scrabble game, yellow Post-it pad, and two pens. I told the cashier that I would come back for all the furniture, as soon as I made a friend to help me.

When I came home to my new place, satisfied that I had got only what I needed, with just a few small gifts to myself, I put the finished Scrabble game in the middle of the living room floor, tossed the six-pack in the fridge, and began reading over a To Do list with my dry pen in hand. At some point, I cracked an empty beer and looked out the window, thinking that I was maybe going to make it, this time, in this new place. Then, there was a knock on the door, but, whoever it was, they were already leaving.

Acknowledgments

I am pleased to publicly thank the many people who supported my writing, across the country and through the years. I want to thank the editors of the magazines who originally published these stories in slightly different form:

Adirondack Review: "Kind Eyes";
The American Scholar: "Out of Order";
Bellow Literary Journal: "Test";
Crossborder: "Unidentified Living Object";
Dogwood: "A Proper Hunger";
Gingko Tree Review: "The Mime";
The Pinch: "Ready Set";
Pindeldyboz: "Camp Redo";
The Southern Review: "Complicated and Annoying Little Robot," "Giant," and "The OK End of Funny Town";
Tahoma Literary Review: "An Exact Thing";
Third Coast: "Gracie";
Unlikely Stories: "Used Goods";
Wag's Revue: "Genie" and "Porcelain God."

"Giant" was reprinted in *Best American Nonrequired Reading 2017* (Houghton Mifflin Harcourt, 2017).

"Porcelain God" and an excerpt of "Ready Set," which originally appeared in *POP!*, are included in this collection courtesy of Stillhouse Press.

I am forever indebted to the professors in the English Department at Skidmore College and the MFA Program at the University of Arizona, especially Aurelie Sheehan, Elizabeth Evans, Greg Hrbek, Jason Brown, and Kathryn Davis. Many thanks to the writers at the UA workshop, especially Cara Adams, Donald Dunbar, Isaac Eldridge, Jamie Poissant, Lisa Ciccarello, and William Bert. Thank you to Peter Conners and the team at BOA for believing in this book. I am grateful to John Murray and Will MacLaughlin, who have been reading my stories from the get-go. Rachel Yoder, thank you for being my greatest ally in all this. Dave Polanzak and Henrietta Polanzak, your relentless encouragement sustains me. Steven Millhauser, thank you for giving me my writing life. And lastly, thank you, Alle, for your love and our life together.

About the Author

Mark Polanzak is author of the hybrid work, *POP!* (George Mason University/Stillhouse Press). His stories have appeared in *Best American Nonrequired Reading, The American Scholar, The Southern Review, Third Coast, The Pinch*, and elsewhere. He is a founding editor for *draft: the journal of process*, and a contributor to The Fail Safe podcast. A graduate of the University of Arizona's MFA program in fiction, he teaches writing and literature at the Berklee College of Music in Boston. Mark lives with his wife near the ocean in Salem, Massachusetts, where he thinks up and works on stories at the coffee shops and bars.

BOA Editions, Ltd.
American Reader Series

No. 1   Christmas at the Four Corners
        of the Earth
        Prose by Blaise Cendrars
        Translated by Bertrand
        Mathieu

No. 2   Pig Notes & Dumb Music:
        Prose on Poetry
        By William Heyen

No. 3   After-Images:
        Autobiographical Sketches
        By W. D. Snodgrass

No. 4   Walking Light: Memoirs and
        Essays on Poetry
        By Stephen Dunn

No. 5   To Sound Like Yourself: Essays
        on Poetry
        By W. D. Snodgrass

No. 6   You Alone Are Real to Me:
        Remembering Rainer Maria
        Rilke
        By Lou Andreas-Salomé

No. 7   Breaking the Alabaster Jar:
        Conversations with Li-Young
        Lee
        Edited by Earl G. Ingersoll

No. 8   I Carry A Hammer In My
        Pocket For Occasions
        Such As These
        By Anthony Tognazzini

No. 9   Unlucky Lucky Days
        By Daniel Grandbois

No. 10 Glass Grapes and Other
        Stories
        By Martha Ronk

No. 11 Meat Eaters & Plant Eaters
        By Jessica Treat

No. 12 On the Winding Stair
        By Joanna Howard

No. 13 Cradle Book
        By Craig Morgan Teicher

No. 14 In the Time of the Girls
        By Anne Germanacos

No. 15 This New and Poisonous Air
        By Adam McOmber

No. 16 To Assume a Pleasing Shape
        By Joseph Salvatore

No. 17 The Innocent Party
        By Aimee Parkison

No. 18 Passwords Primeval: 20
        American Poets in Their Own
        Words
        Interviews by Tony Leuzzi

No. 19 The Era of Not Quite
        By Douglas Watson

No. 20 The Winged Seed: A
        Remembrance
        By Li-Young Lee

No. 21 Jewelry Box: A Collection of
        Histories
        By Aurelie Sheehan

No. 22 The Tao of Humiliation
        By Lee Upton

No. 23 Bridge
        By Robert Thomas

No. 24 Reptile House
        By Robin McLean

No. 25 The Education of a Poker
        Player
        James McManus

No. 26 Remarkable
        By Dinah Cox

No. 27 Gravity Changes
        By Zach Powers

No. 28 My House Gathers Desires
        By Adam McOmber

Colophon

BOA Editions, Ltd., a not-for-profit publisher of poetry and other literary works, fosters readership and appreciation of contemporary literature. By identifying, cultivating, and publishing both new and established poets and selecting authors of unique literary talent, BOA brings high-quality literature to the public. Support for this effort comes from the sale of its publications, grant funding, and private donations.

The publication of this book is made possible, in part, by the special support of the following individuals:

Anonymous
June C. Baker
Angela Bonazinga & Catherine Lewis
James Long Hale
Art & Pam Hatton
Jack & Gail Langerak
Joe McElveney
Boo Poulin
Steven O. Russell & Phyllis Rifkin-Russell
David W. Ryon
Meredith & Adam Smith
Sue S. Stewart, *in memory of Steven L. Raymond*
William Waddell & Linda Rubel